love you ALWAYS

AVA HUNTER

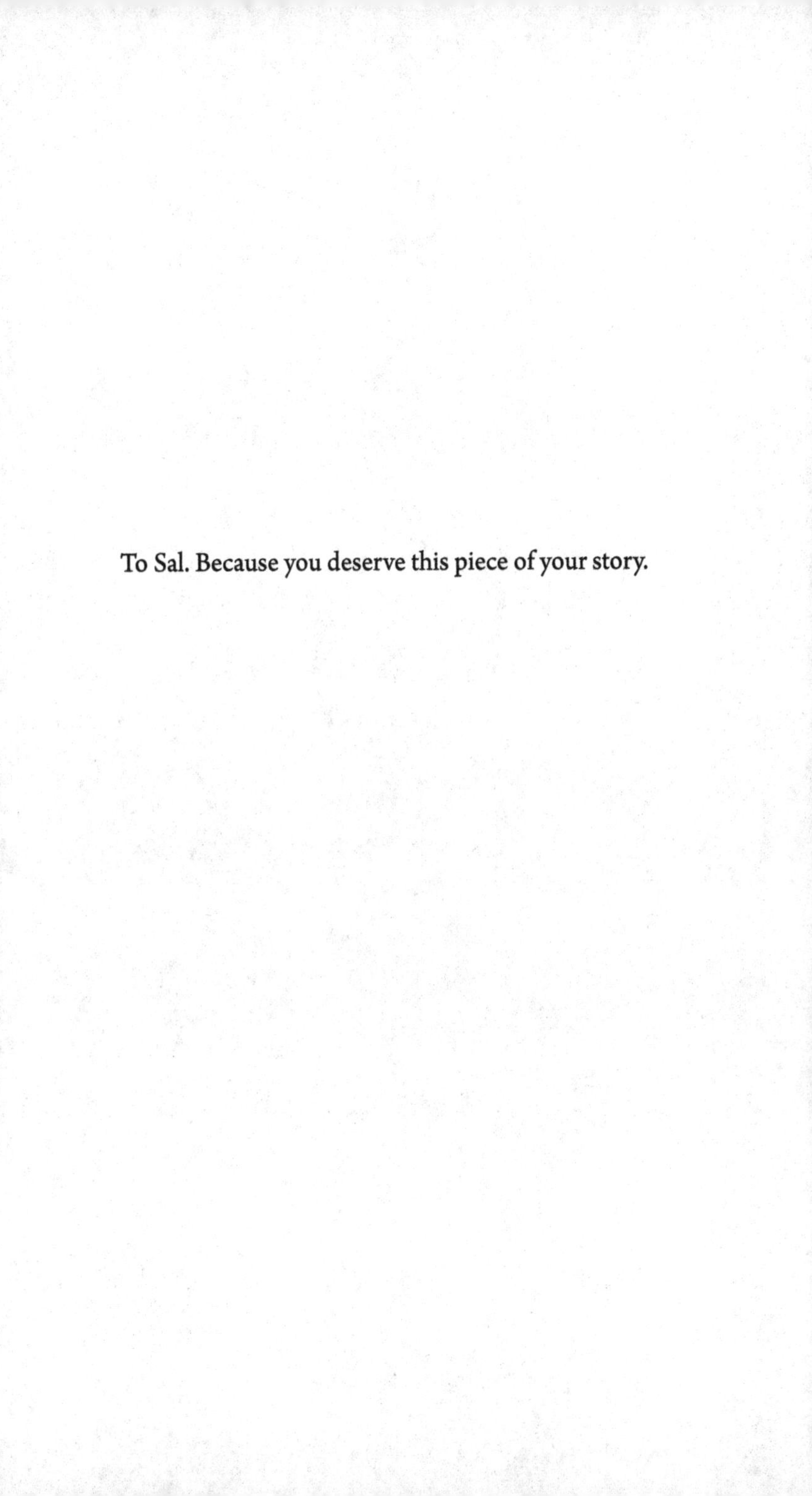
To Sal. Because you deserve this piece of your story.

chapter
ONE

NO, SHE THINKS. *No, no, no.*

Sal Kincaid sits in the bathroom stall, staring at the dark smear on the inside of her underwear. She bites her lip, frustration building in her until she finally wipes, flushes the evidence and stands.

Another month, another hope down the literal drain.

With a heavy sigh, Sal exits the stall. She washes her hands, the water warm over her trembling fingers, and dries them on scratchy paper. She meets her reflection in the mirror and winces.

She has to tell Luke.

Again.

There's still no baby. And at the rate they're going there might never be. For the last year they've been trying. With the exception of her first pregnancy, she's never made it past eight weeks. Sure, a few stuck, but they all ended the same. In blood. In loss.

She never thought it would be this hard. She and Luke had had enough heartbreak, she thought the universe would cut her a break, make wishing for a tiny baby easy, but it's like running headlong into a brick wall over and over again.

A voice over the hospital loudspeaker calls for Doctor Yates. Sal takes down the loose braid she wears. As much a part of her uniform as the starchy paramedic garb she sports. She combs her fingers through the dark strands and gives herself a get-your-shit-together scowl in the mirror. She's a fighter.

After all the hard knocks on the baby front, she has to remind herself about everything she has. All she has to be grateful for. Her life, for instance.

It was only two years ago that Sal was in a plane crash, leaving her friends and family to think she was dead. She was left with no memory. Left living with a madman who manipulated her into believing he was her husband for nine months. But then Luke found her. And he brought her back to their life—and their love.

She and Luke—they've overcome so much. Both before her memory loss and after.

Henry.

Sal closes her eyes. The name of her first baby, a baby she miscarried at four months in an awful car accident before she went missing, haunts her. She can't remember him. And it kills her. It absolutely kills her.

Shaking her head, she chases away the weary thought. Better to focus on all the good things in her life. Everything she's rebuilt. Everything she can hold on to. Her health. Her friends and family. Her job.

Slowly but surely, she was able to recertify her paramedic's license. Her skills, her knowledge, held innate for so long, became automatic the second she started classes. It was like muscle memory. Like a blessing. And though her memory still hasn't fully returned, Sal's been determined to live her life to the fullest. This is just her life now and she's okay with it.

She's fucking Sal Kincaid and she came back from the goddamn dead.

Exhaling a resolute breath, Sal opens her eyes and wipes a long strand of chocolate-brown hair away from her face. *Let's go home*, she thinks to herself as she exits the bathroom and walks down the long hallway of the hospital.

After staying with a patient for the last three hours until they were admitted, she's bone-tired. Ready to get home. A glass of wine. A shower. Luke. A smile tugs at her lips. Even now, miles apart, he still has her knees going weak. Sal never knew you could crave a person. Food, sure. Sleep, definitely. But Luke. He's a soul quench. A fierce force of love. And at the end of a long day, there's nothing better than the sight of her hot-as-hell husband taking her in his strong arms and bending her over—

"Whoa, sweetcheeks, where you goin'?"

Sal's jolted to a stop as a hand snags her arm. Tawny Reynolds, the other half of her paramedic team, stands in front of her. All biceps and black-ink tattoos, Tawny's a boss. She takes no shit, and she and Sal always have each other's backs when it comes time to step up.

"Home," Sal says, giving her partner a smile. "You know, that warm and cozy place where relaxation beckons."

Tawny shrugs. "Can't say I've heard of it."

Sal laughs. "That's because you live in a gym."

"Truth." Tawny cocks her head. "You finally get that patient admitted?"

"Yeah. Only took three hours." She moves to the side,

getting out of the traffic of the hallway, and Tawny follows suit.

"Damn." Tawny shakes her golden lion's mane of hair. "That's rough. Which is why I feel like an asshole for asking this right now."

Sal lifts a brow. "What's up?"

"I need a really big favor. Nurse Buntin's got a patient in exam room two who's clamming up."

Sal sighs, knowing what Tawny wants. She thinks of Luke, on his way home from the studio. Though her husband's been nothing but supportive since she went back to work months ago, he worries when she's late. A throwback to last year. A never-healed wound from when Sal went missing.

Tawny's brown eyes are all apologies. "I know you're on your way home to your handsome husband but . . . please? No one can get her to talk. And we all know about that magic touch of yours."

Sal smiles slightly. Since she's been back on the job, she's learned she has a rep around the hospital as someone who takes their time with the patients. Makes them feel as comfortable as possible. Having firsthand experience with hospital stays, she knows it's important for them to be listened to and understood even while in their most painful moments.

Tawny's serious face morphs into a pleading smile. "Pretty please?"

"Fine," Sal groans but grins back at her. "Lead the way."

Through the exam room window, Sal sees a young girl, huddled in a corner chair, her legs pulled up to her chest. She's waifish with a short red pixie cut and a wary expression. Nurse Buntin leans over, giving Sal the details. "Molly Banks. Twenty-two. She was brought in complaining of stomach pain but now won't let anyone examine her."

Sal nods. She's seen her share of noncompliant patients. Most lie because they're embarrassed to tell the truth, or want to avoid being judged or scolded. It's her job to coax the truth out of them so they can be safely treated.

"Molly?" Sal says as she enters the room.

The girl looks up, her face full of bewilderment.

"Hi, my name's Sal and I'm a paramedic." Molly watches with suspicious eyes as Sal walks further into the exam room. "I hear you're having some trouble. I don't blame you. No one likes it here."

The girl's face softens.

"Nurse Buntin says you came in with stomach pain. You want to tell me about it?"

"Not really."

"Are you sure?" As she gets closer, a familiar chill steals over Sal. Though Molly's tried to cover it with makeup, her right eye is black and blue. Sal's eyes drift. More bruises. On her wrists this time.

A long pause. Molly tightens her arms around her legs, resting her chin on her knees. "I feel better now. Really. I can go home."

"Well, we'd hate to send you home if something was wrong." Sal kneels beside the chair. She keeps a soft voice. "Are you here because of that eye?"

Molly shifts uncomfortably. "No."

"Because if you are, there's nothing wrong with that."

Molly doesn't reply, staring off into space, her attention diverted elsewhere.

The girl's a wall, and Sal needs to break through.

She searches her mind and has the answer. It's not her favorite, but it's honest. And hopefully, it will work.

Taking a breath, chasing away the nerves bubbling up, Sal forces herself back to the past. "Believe me, I've been where you have."

Molly squints at Sal, her stare disbelieving. "I doubt that," she sniffs. Her face is like a wounded animal, distrustful, bitter.

Sal nods. "I have. It was about two years ago and it was awful. I was with a man who didn't treat me right at all. Who hurt me."

Molly lifts her head, straightening up.

"There were days when I didn't want to exist, days when I didn't know what to do, when I felt all alone." She licks her lips. Her throat wants to shut down at the words she's saying, because they feel foreign—they're not her life anymore—but she pushes past it. Pushes herself. "Finally, I made the decision to get out, and it was hard, Molly. So damn hard. It won't be easy for you, but I understand what you're going through. I really do."

Molly's gaze tracks Sal, a small flicker of belief beneath her hard exterior.

Sal's breath is held tight in her chest. She hopes Molly's listening. As she meets the girl's brown-eyed gaze, she says, "No one's saying you have to do anything now. All I want to do is make sure you're okay. That's what's important."

Molly shakes her head, thinking on it, worrying, but then she whispers, suddenly, "He doesn't know I'm here.

"Who doesn't?"

Her eyes well. "My husband. Chris. He found out I'm

pregnant. And . . ." Molly trails off. Unfurling her legs, she lifts her shirt. What Sal sees has her blood turning to fire. The imprint of a shoe sole branded on Molly's stomach. "He doesn't want me to have it. Doesn't want there to be anyone else." She draws her legs back up, closing herself off. "I don't want it either. I can't. I can't have it."

A pang hits Sal at the mention of a baby, a baby no one wants, but she checks her own feelings, her judgment. What Molly's saying is horrifying, but Sal lets her talk. The girl needs to get it out, needs someone to listen to her, because right now, as Sal knows, Molly's mindset is that this is normal. That she's the one who did something wrong.

Molly stares at Sal. Hurt in her eyes. "And the cops don't help. They always come but they never listen to me. They leave me there. They don't do a thing."

"I understand," Sal says carefully. "They didn't help me very much either." She smiles even though it takes all her strength. "How about I help you?" She holds Molly's eyes. She can see the girl relenting, giving in to someone who gives a damn.

"I'm scared." Her eyes dart to Nurse Buntin, who's hovering in the hall. "I don't want to be alone."

"You won't be. I'll be right there with you."

She sniffles. "You will?"

"Of course I will." Sal wants to give this girl just a moment of tenderness. Hell, she once was this girl. Trapped with Roy. Desperate. Confused. The memory is ruthless and Sal's stomach churns. Everything from the past rushing back, hitting her hard like a rogue wave, ready to wreak havoc.

Molly shifts on the chair. "No needles?"

Sal chuckles. "No needles."

"And you won't go?"

"No, I won't."

But she thinks of Luke at home. Wondering. Worrying.

"I just need one second, okay?" Standing, she pats Molly's hand. "How about you hop up on that table and I'll be right back?"

As Molly reluctantly climbs up on the table, Sal steps outside the room. After giving Nurse Buntin a brief rundown on Molly's condition so far, she says, "I'll stay for the exam. Make sure she gets through it okay."

"You're a saint."

Ducking into a corner of the hall, Sal pulls out her phone to send a quick text to Luke.

She smiles, her heart lifting as she writes the words.

I'm late tonight. I love you. Bet you a beer I still beat you home.

Luke Kincaid kicks up a boot on his knee and leans back against the studio couch, eyeing the track list he holds in his hand. With swift decision, he draws arrows between two songs. "We should swap the order of 'In Country We Trust' and 'Nice Shot.'"

Seth, his younger brother, grins at him. "You're worryin' about the order and we still gotta record the damn songs, man."

Jace, wearing a face of equal concentration, arcs a brow as he stares at the track list. "I mean, if Luke wants to get sadder with it, we can get sadder with it."

"Goin' for the gold," Seth drawls.

Luke nods. "Goin' for number one."

His gaze drifts around the room, taking in the mess they've made over the course of a ten-hour day. Guitars leaned up against the walls. Microphones. Amplifiers. Beer cans. All the fixings signaling a wrap on the first day of their Saturday jam session.

A surge of pride swells in Luke's chest. The Brothers Kincaid just finished a grueling five-month arena tour. They've been back in Nashville for less than a month and already they're scribbling new songs for their eighth album. It's as if after being on hiatus for a year, Luke's moving as fast as he can to get the Brothers Kincaid to play catch-up.

The ping of his cell phone has Luke grabbing it up. He smiles seeing Sal's name pop up on the screen. But the smile's short-lived as he reads the message from his wife.

I'm late tonight. I love you. Bet you a beer I still beat you home.

The text hits him like a fist to the gut.

He's worrying. And he shouldn't. Sal's strong. Sal's fine. Working too damn much but fine. After months of being on the road with Sal by his side, being without her is a foreign concept. He doesn't like it. Not one damn bit.

A string twangs from the corner of the room where Seth is packing up his fiddle.

Luke texts back: *Be safe. Love you too.*

Sal would kick his ass if she knew how much he worried, how much he still feared losing her. It's his crutch. The loss of Sal.

It's been over a year since Sal faced down Roy in their kitchen. Another haunting scene to add to Luke's memories.

He still sees Sal on their kitchen floor. Unmoving, crumpled like a broken doll. At times, the image has the power to take him from his music, his thoughts, his sleep. Steal the air from his chest. If he hadn't made it downstairs in time . . .

But he did.

And Sal fought for herself, for their love, and won. She suffered so much, and still, she came up swinging.

The word *strong* doesn't even do his wife justice.

Since then, they've both been walking their road. Together. Luke's been making up for lost time. Lost time with the music. Lost time with Sal.

He checks the clock on the wall, tuning out Seth and Jace's conversation about next month's gig at Ace's Saloon.

He needs to get home. Pick up a bottle of wine and some flowers and have a night just him and Sal. No distractions. They've both been batshit busy since they got back from tour. He has to make more time for her. Can't fall back into old patterns. Nothing comes before his wife—especially not the music.

Even his current country music superstar status feels like a dream. It seems so long ago he was a shell of a man; the Brothers Kincaid a shell of a band. For almost a year, after Sal had disappeared in the plane crash, Luke had a death wish. He didn't want to live if his wife didn't. But all that changed when Seth found Sal in Florida. His wife was alive, being held by Roy, a madman in a Florida shack, her memory gone. By some miracle she had come back to him. But Luke had his secrets about their past. He wanted to protect Sal while she healed, but in doing so, he only made things worse.

When she found out, learned about the kiss between

him and Alabama, the baby she'd miscarried, he was sure he had lost her. By some grace, she forgave him, and they came back stronger than ever.

Hell, sometimes he can't believe he deserves her. He can't believe how goddamn lucky he is that she's his.

"Earth to Luke."

At the sound of his brother's low rumble, he looks up and over.

Seth leans against the wall. "Welcome back, man," he says, waving the scribbled-on list of songs.

Luke blows out a breath, trying to shake off his concern about Sal. "What'd I miss?"

"I was askin' if we're really doin' a collab with Griff Greyson." Seth crosses his arms, a withering scowl on his usually easy-going face.

"Yeah. We really are."

Seth sighs. Long and loud.

Jace snickers. "Someone's got the theatrics down pat."

Seth scoffs, affronted. "Can you blame me?"

Luke chuckles. Seth's made no effort to hide his dislike of Griff. The guy rubs Seth the wrong way, and while Luke at times finds him abrasive, he likes Griff despite their rocky start.

Seth shakes his head, not letting it go. "You're backin' the wrong horse, Luke. Album's gonna tank."

Luke runs a hand down his chin, considering it. "Now I ain't so sure about that."

Months ago, Griff tapped Luke to do a duet on his solo album and it's Luke's turn to return the favor. But he ain't doing it to be nice. He's being honest. Griff's a damn good singer, he likes the guy, and he's saying so.

Still, it's a group effort. Luke surveys his band. Seth glowering. Jace contemplative. "What about you?" he asks his best friend. "You wanna weigh in?"

Jace scratches his jaw. "I think it's a solid idea." Seth groans. Jace continues. "He's an asshole, but he can sing. Why not?" He nods at Luke. "He'd move some records, no doubt."

Seth tosses Jace a dry look at being outvoted. "Thanks for stayin' on your bullshit, Jace."

Jace's solemn face turns to a smirk. "Anytime."

The decision made by his band, Luke nods, standing. He grabs up his guitar and gently places it in his case.

"Headed home?" Seth asks.

"Not yet. Got some stops on the way. Sal ain't home till late."

Seth's eyes flicker. "She's workin' a lot."

Luke snaps the clasps on the guitar case. "Too much."

Jace drops onto a stool. "You ever think about askin' her to quit?"

Seth busts out a laugh. "Have you met Sal?"

"Yeah, I like my nuts where they are, thanks," Luke says, half-kidding, half-knowing he would never ask that of Sal. It's her job, it's important to her, and she's got his support. Anytime. All the time.

The soft suck of the door has Luke turning.

Their manager, Bobby Mazon, enters the room wearing a clumsy step and a neon jacket. While Mort was all finesse and money, Bobby's about as smooth as sandpaper.

Bobby whistles and shuts the door behind him. "Day one's a wrap, gentlemen. How do we feel?"

Luke lets out a low whoop. "Feelin' damn good, Bobby."

"Hey, Bobby, man," Jace says, a smile turning his lips. "You got your tie on upside down."

Bobby blinks, then swivels his hand over to his polka-dotted bowtie.

Seth shoots Luke a what-the-hell-are-we-doing-with-this-guy look, but Luke can only chuckle. Sure, their new manager is a walking space case, but he's a good guy. Where Mort would steamroll the Brothers Kincaid into a decision, Bobby's content to let them lead, but also offers sound advice when needed.

Sometimes Luke still can't believe everything that went down with Mort. Setting Alabama up to kiss him so he'd stay on as a client. Arranging that damn *Nashville Star* photographer to take the photo that ultimately caused Sal's car accident and miscarriage. Though Mort got what was coming from him—fired by his clients, his reputation ruined—he still got the hell out of Nashville as fast as he could run.

Luke's fists curl at the thought. Some small part of him wishes Mort were still around, if only so he could beat the shit out of the guy one last time.

Bobby chatters on. "A word, Luke?"

"What's up?"

"So I know you fellas got the *Rolling Stone* interview Tuesday, but I got somethin' just for you. PR op. *Country Living* wants you and Sal for an interview." Lifting a hand, Bobby squints at the note scribbled onto his palm. "A cover about great country love stories."

A shit-eating grin appears on Seth's face. He's ready to bust his brother's balls as only he can do. "Pucker up, Luke."

But Luke bristles. A frown creases his brow.

He's had more than his share of the press. Especially

after Sal was found. The media was all over her, harassing her, trying for a story, mainly the *Nashville Star*, the local tabloid. Even now, a year after everything, Sal's still somewhat of a media darling. Beautiful. Tragic. Strong. Everyone wants a piece of her, wants to know more, which only has Luke fighting to keep their life private as much as he can.

Though he'll always do an interview for himself, or the band, Sal's out of the spotlight unless it's her call.

"I don't know. I don't like puttin' Sal out there, Bobby." He runs a thoughtful hand through his hair, then shakes his head. "Give it to someone else."

Where Mort would argue, Bobby only nods.

Seth laughs when Luke glances his way. He holds up his hands. "Hey, don't look at me."

Luke eyes Jace. "What about you?"

Jace laughs. "Give Emmy Lou a cover? Hell, she'll be thrilled." His rusty brows rise. "You sure, though?"

He catches the look Seth's giving him, then gives a terse nod. "Yeah. You take it," he says, grabbing up his guitar case. He floats a wave. "See y'all tomorrow."

"Tomorrow," Jace echoes, lifting a hand.

Seth swaggers. "Can't promise anything. Got a date. We're goin' to church."

"Oh, we're calling Tonk's Church again?" Jace quips.

Luke rolls his eyes. Seth just keeps the mischievous grin on his face.

"Sunday supper," he tells his brother in a hard, no-bullshit tone. "Don't miss it."

It's important to Sal. Sunday suppers. The one day of the week their close-knit group of friends gets together to eat, drink and sing. Since she's been back it's been her way of finding herself, her slice of normalcy.

He strides across the room and pauses in the doorway. "Sal'll kill ya. Then I'll kick your ass. Then she'll kill you again."

Seth laughs. But his eyes are soft. He knows how much it means to Sal. "I'll be there, man. Relax."

Relax.

Right.

Luke exits the studio, his boots stomping hard down the hall. His heart thundering. His mind on his wife and making it home to her.

chapter
TWO

S AL FLICKS ON THE SOFT LIGHT OF THE KITCHEN, instantly illuminating the messy countertop. The way she and Luke left it this morning in their hasty exit. Her forgotten thermos of coffee. Cereal bowls stacked in the sink. Crumpled *Nashville Stars*. A quick survey around, a quick call out tells her that Luke's not yet home from the studio. A small smile graces her face. He and Seth probably got to bullshitting.

Sal's stomach rumbles as she tosses her keys in the small tray, cracks a window and checks the fridge. She forgot to eat lunch, and although she's starving, the thought of whipping up dinner is already exhausting. She's exhausted. The entire drive home, she kept thinking of Molly. Though the girl never explicitly admitted her husband did anything, she hopes she was given the resources to get help.

Shutting the fridge, Sal leans back against the counter. She lets out a tired sigh but smiles as she takes in her beloved farmhouse. Lit up with warm light. A cool summer breeze wafting through the window. But as her eyes land on a particular spot of cracked tile, Sal can't help the icy chill that zips up her spine. She closes her eyes to fight it off, but her mind's already going there. Back to the boogeyman. Back to over a year ago when Roy Williams, the monster who had held her captive, came to their home and attacked her and Luke both.

Sal fought and finally won, driving Luke's broken guitar stake through the bastard's neck.

Luke wanted to move, but Sal was adamant they stay in their home. Every single thing in the farmhouse, they had built it together. This home is their heart. She could feel it the second she set foot inside, even if she couldn't remember the past. She'd never let Roy chase her away from her life. Never again. Not even for the blood spilled. The bad memories. Her and Luke—they'd build new. Better.

A floorboard in the house creaks.

A hitch of her breath, her heart.

Then she's letting out a sigh of relief when she sees Luke in the doorway. A bottle of wine's tucked under his arm. In his other hand, he carries a pizza, a bouquet of gorgeous magenta peonies balanced on top of it.

"Damn," he says, looking crestfallen. "You beat me."

Sal laughs, her face heating at the sight of her tall, tan country boy. He looks adorably haggard, his dark hair mussed, the perfect amount of scruff dusting his face. The sleeves of his blue jean shirt are shoved up to the elbows, exposing tan arms corded with lean muscle.

She arches a brow. "Was there ever any doubt?"

Grinning, he takes a stride across the kitchen, depositing everything in his arms on the counter before sweeping her into his embrace. "Hell, I'm sorry, darlin.'" His hands tenderly cup her face, his thumbs grazing her cheek. "I was rushin' home . . . I wanted to surprise you."

Her heart warms at his words. "Well, you did. This is perfect. You come bearing all the things I could ever want. Wine. Pizza. Flowers." She stands on tiptoes to kiss him. "You."

They come together like magnets. Sal sighs, drinking in his scent, the heady, familiar smell of wood shavings and rosewood oil. Luke's mouth travels from her lips to the curve of her neck. His long fingers deftly unbutton the top button of her uniform. "I missed you."

"I missed you too." Sal reaches down to palm the front of his pants, finding a rock-hard erection. She smiles. "Mmm. You must have really missed me . . ."

"I can't help it," Luke breathes into her hair. "You look so goddamn sexy in your uniform."

Sal chuckles as Luke tugs on her top. A tug that tells her he'll soon be tearing it off like so many others before it. "You know," she murmurs, "you ruin this uniform, I can't get anoth—"

Sal gasps as Luke crushes her mouth with a toe-curling kiss. The best kind of kiss where everything disappears for just a moment. Where you're reminded just how much you matter.

Sal wraps her arms around his neck and arcs into him. Every bit of her is white-hot. Every bit of her body is a go. For Luke. Always for Luke.

"You hungry?" he asks between kisses. Asks even as he's slipping her top off her shoulder.

"Food can wait." Sal grazes her mouth against his jaw. His stubbled cheek scratches her palm, their tattoo. She relishes the feeling. The lifeforce of Luke.

That's when she remembers. She braces a hand on his shoulder. "I can't."

"What is it?" he asks.

She hesitates, hating to ruin the moment, but whispers, "I'm spotting. It should be fine, but . . ."

"Don't you worry about that, darlin.'" His dark, attentive eyes flash with worry but he doesn't miss a beat. His eyes tell her they'll talk after. That right now he's going to do everything in his power to make her forget their troubles. "Let me worry about you."

For a second, Sal can barely breathe, overcome with emotion. When all feels lost, Luke is there. He gives her everything and she can't fathom how much he loves her. Or maybe she can. Because she loves him back just as hard.

Falling in love with Luke all over again has been the easiest and the best thing she's ever done.

A warm body rush overtakes Sal as Luke backs her up against the kitchen table. He kneels before her, his fingers curling around her waistband. Impatiently, he drags off her pants, then her panties, tossing them across the room.

His broad palm slips between her legs, moving up her thigh as he kisses himself up her legs, lean legs she knows he loves, kisses her sex, her slim waist. Then, he grips her thighs hard, primal, and stands. His hands slide over her shoulders, a soft, teasing caress, and that's when he tears at her top. Sal cries out in delight as buttons skitter across the room. Luke pulls her shirt off, and then her bra.

Cool air puckers her nipples. He dips his head to take a pink bud in his mouth. She grips the table edge to keep herself standing, to keep herself together. Damn near ready to lose her mind at the way Luke tastes her. Feasting on her. Like he can't get enough. Never enough.

Her heart thumping, Sal lets Luke take her in his arms and set her down on the edge of the kitchen table. A slight thrill goes through her. Everything about this is illicit and improper and Sal can't get enough. They're like lovers, like teenagers, only it's her kitchen and her husband and she's going to enjoy every damn second of it.

Without missing a beat, Luke leans over and shuts off the light. His smile's roguish as he stares down at her. "Don't want anyone else seein' you but me."

Luke trails hot kisses along her collarbone, cupping her breast in his palm. Sal shivers from the sensation. Her country boy with his gentle hands, calloused fingertips circling her nipple, bringing it to a hardened bud. Sal makes a small sound, her body arching up into Luke's.

He catches her in his arms, bringing her against him. And then he stops and says, "God, you're beautiful." He's staring at her. His dark eyes dazed with lust. Ravenous. A warm blush creeps across her face. She's never gotten used to Luke's stare. While she loves it, she doesn't know what she's done to deserve it. He looks at her like she's a goddess. Some impossible savior when all she feels like these days is an absolute failure of a woman.

Sal responds by lurching, crushing Luke's mouth with hers, winding her arms around his neck as his hands find her down below. His long fingers dip into her with a gentle probe. One, then two, then her sweet spot. Luke growls, at the slickness of her arousal, at her whimper of pleasure, and grips her even tighter, his body a massive wall against her petite frame.

Sal releases a low moan. He's teasing her. Flat out tormenting her with his honeyed touch. Finally, she can't take it any longer. "Please, Luke."

She says his name and it's like a pistol start. His dark eyes flash at the begging tremble in her voice.

He unzips his jeans, letting them fall to his ankles.

Luke lays her down on the table. He drapes his lean frame over her, one arm gripping the edge of the table above her, the other down by her side, joining their palms, their tattoos forming their final sentences: ALL THE ROADS LEAD TO US.

Slowly, he pushes into her.

Sal gasps. She'll never get used to the sensation of him. Hard and throbbing, every part of him showing her how bad he wants her. How much he needs her.

"Goddamn," Luke grits out, his breath hot near her ear. "Sal, you feel so fuckin' good."

His voice, desperate, haggard, has her writhing, wanting to feel him.

Luke undulates in a slow roll of a movement. Like a wave of friction cresting over Sal. She shifts with him, rocking her body against his. Her legs wrap around his waist and she pulls him in closer. Deeper.

Sal closes her eyes, losing herself in his grip, his movements.

Her anchor. Her rock.

Luke.

Sal wraps an arm around his neck, digging her nails into his sculpted shoulder. "Faster," she whispers.

With a primal groan, Luke thrusts, driving into her.

Soft moonlight spills through the kitchen window.

The table rocks with the weight of their bodies but holds steady.

Sal pants in his ear. Luke grips the table edge, so strong it's a wonder he doesn't pick the table up and them right along with it. Her body flushes with warmth as Sal feels that familiar lick of fire travel from her toes up her spine. A release. A bright, brilliant bonfire building behind her eyes and down below.

"Yes, yes," Sal gasps. "Together. Together, Luke."

He nods, his face buried in her hair. His breath shaking out in a desperate pant as he plows harder, thrusts deeper.

Sal's body's a rocket, shooting up to the stars, to sparkling light. To something greater than herself. To her and Luke. Her road.

A roar rips forth from Luke's mouth. He shudders as he spills into her, Sal's own satisfied cry echoing in the darkened kitchen.

Sighing, Sal threads her fingers through Luke's dark hair. Luke remains as he is, buried in her, his eyes closed, his breathing steady and content. He kisses her temple, his next words a desperate plea. Hoarse with infinite promise. "I love you, Sal. So damn much."

Sal closes her eyes. "I love you too," she whispers.

Luke straightens up, chuckling as he evaluates the war-torn kitchen. He eyes his wife. The gorgeous cause of it all.

Christ, he wanted her so damn bad. He walked in that kitchen, intent on surprising her with food and flowers, and instead found himself rock-hard when he found Sal's teasing eyes bidding him to come closer. Looking so damn sexy in her uniform. So powerful and take charge. He could've torn this fucking house apart with his bare hands to get to her.

And he damn near did.

His eyes move back to Sal, who's sitting up on the table, a content smile on her full lips. "You want a shower, darlin'?" he asks, hitching up his jeans

"No," she says with a tilt of her dark head. "Let's stay here. Have a picnic."

He steps away from Sal long enough to grab an afghan off the couch. He returns, wrapping it around her and helping her off the table. Wordlessly, she smiles her thanks, then sinks to the floor.

"What do you say?" Luke swipes the pizza and the bottle of wine from the counter. "Think we worked up enough of an appetite?"

"I'd say so." Sal raises her palms like a prayer as Luke lowers himself to the floor with the provisions. "Cold pizza and wine? Heaven sent."

They settle back against the cabinets for support. Pizza slices are stolen from the box. The wine's uncorked. Sal wears the blanket like a dress, tucked under her arms, looking so damn beautiful it's a wonder he doesn't lay her down for round two. He can't help his lingering gaze. She's tan from the sun, from her long runs around the farm property, her dark hair glossy and tangled.

This is what he wants. Sitting in the kitchen, eating cold pizza, drinking wine from the bottle. What he and Sal dreamed about. It could be any town, anywhere, drinking champagne or cheap beer, but the damn truth is being together is what it was about.

Luke passes the bottle between them. Sal drinks from it, glances around the moonlit kitchen. "I'm glad we can still do this."

Though her words are light, airy, something unspoken passes between them. Luke understands what she means. Last year, a man was killed in their kitchen. They should have moved. Should have burned the place to the ground. And yet they didn't. Him and Sal, they've rebuilt. They can't forget but they can move on. They have to.

Sal wipes her lips on her bare arm. Her emerald eyes shine in the dim light of the kitchen. "How was your day?"

Luke stretches out on the floor, his back resting against a cupboard. "Pretty damn great, actually. We wrote a few new songs. Bobby's huntin' us up a new producer for the album. Gotta be someone fuckin' fantastic seein' as it's number eight."

Her eyes widen. "Already?"

"Already." He chuckles. "Seth's bitchin' about Griff Greyson bein' on the album. Thinks the album will tank."

"Luke," Sal chides softly. "You guys don't know how to make a bad song." She hugs him to her. "What else?"

"Got that interview with *Rolling Stone* on Tuesday."

Sal tips her head to his shoulder. "We're busy."

"We are. How 'bout you?" He glances close at Sal's moonlit profile. She looks tired. Fragile. "You want to tell me about today? Looks like it was rough."

He saw it on her face when he walked into the kitchen. Damn near exhausted from something. What, he doesn't know, but he damn sure wants to find out.

Straightening up, Sal blows out a breath and curls into him. "It was. It was a hard day. There was this girl there. She wasn't even my patient, but she wouldn't talk to anyone else. She was trying to hide the fact that she was pregnant." Luke's breath stalls, but Sal goes on. "She had these bruises, all over her arms, her stomach, and I knew, I just knew . . ."

As she trails off, a long-buried but always present fury overtakes Luke. He doesn't know how Sal managed to keep it together today, because at the mention, it's taking all Luke has not to crumble, to give in to his anger. Any man who hurts a woman doesn't deserve to live. It still has Luke wanting to kill Roy, even though the bastard's already dead, over and over and over again.

Sal's voice has gone distant and sad, pulling Luke's focus back to his wife.

"It had me remembering Roy. I wanted to stay and help her. That's why I was late. I thought I could change the world." She shakes her head. "We gave her all the resources to get help, but I . . . I just don't know."

Luke's quiet for a long second.

Sal gives so much, is so damn selfless, it's his job to make sure she takes care of herself.

He turns to her. "Darlin', I love that you wanna help, but I don't want you pushin' yourself too hard. We just got back from tour, and now you're workin' twelve-hour shifts, tryin' to pick up the slack at work."

She cuts him off with a smile. "I haven't had a migraine in months. Or a nightmare. My therapist says I'm making progress." She floats him a smile. "So you should stop worrying. I'm fine."

Fine. That's Sal's code word for *I can do everything*. It was Luke's code word for a damn stubborn woman.

He touches her cheek, wanting her to hear him and not be offended. "You ain't gotta work, you know that."

A soft sigh. "I know."

"But I'd never ask you to stop working either."

"I know that too."

"All I'm sayin' is that you're workin' too much."

"I could say the same thing about you." Sal pulls her legs into her small frame and snuggles into him. "Besides, work helps."

Luke winces. He knows what she means. He's been using his work, his music to bury his own feelings about their inability to get pregnant. So it's no surprise Sal's doing the same.

"Ten months." Sal's soft voice erupts. The words are a thorn. "We've been trying for ten months, Luke. After a year we're infertile." She bites her lip and looks up at him. "Maybe it's time to start thinking about other options?"

His heart clenches at the hope in her eyes. While Luke wants a baby as much Sal does, right now, other options are not an option. At least not for him. After every emotional and physically ravaging thing Sal's been through in the last year, he won't put her through anything else. He doesn't want her to. Maybe in a few years, but not now.

"There ain't no hurry," he says in a quiet voice. "We can go slow. We're young. Healthy."

Sal laughs bitterly. "I know I sound crazy. I just . . . I didn't think it would be this hard when everything else has been so . . ." Her green eyes fill with tears. She shakes her head, her voice a regretful rasp. "I'm so sorry, Luke. I want to give you so much and I just feel like a failure. Like we missed our shot. Like Henry was it and—"

"Hey," he says, his chest aching to the point of pain, knowing how much guilt Sal feels for not remembering the baby she carried for four months. He turns toward her, taking her in his arms, determined not to let her blame herself.

"Don't you apologize. Never for that, you hear me?" His eyes tracing her sorrowful gaze, Luke gently wipes a tear from her cheek. "It ain't your fault. I don't need a baby, Sal, I need you." He gathers her hand in his. "You are the most important piece of my world, darlin'. I don't spin without you in it."

Sal curls against him, burying her face in his chest. "You always know the right thing to say."

Luke swallows, wrapping an arm around her bare shoulders. He hopes so. It hurts him too. All the waiting, then the hope, the heartbreak. But Luke pushes aside his own pain, wanting to be strong for Sal. To show her that while it hurts something fierce, it won't break them or their love. Never.

"Don't worry, you hear me?"

Sal lifts her head. Her eyes glitter with unshed tears. But she nods and smiles soft, cupping the side of his face. "I'll try."

Luke kisses her fiercely. Sal kisses him back, just as fierce. He holds her tight and close, her very form precious, her heartbeat a song against his. A melody only Sal can write.

chapter
THREE

A BOLD SLIVER OF AUGUST SUNLIGHT, BRIGHT, defiant, creeps through the window like a thief of joy. Scowling, Sal cracks an eye and turns on her side to get away from the blinding glare. It's Sunday. Her first day off in over a week and if the sun thinks she's waking up now it's got another thing coming.

A soft chuckle comes from Luke as she tries to burrow into the crook of his arm. "Slay the sun, Luke," she murmurs.

He curves an arm around her head and kisses her temple. "I'll try for you, darlin, but somethin' makes me think it wants us to have the day."

Smiling, she unearths herself from her burrow to see Luke already awake and clear-eyed. One thing she's learned about herself is that even losing her memory can't change the fact that Sal's a sleepyhead, while Luke's a rooster—up at the crack of dawn. In fact, he's probably been up already to feed the animals and then returned to bed.

She leans up to Luke, sweeping her mouth against his. "Good point."

They lie there like that, entwined. Lying in Luke's gentle, yet strong embrace feels like a decadence she doesn't deserve. If she could stay here all day, she'd be content. But then she remembers it's Sunday. While most people detest the end of the week, for Sal, it's her favorite day. When she first returned to Nashville, Seth and Luke told her about their Sunday suppers, their home the hotspot hangout for musicians, friends, and family.

She loves these days. Days where her friends and family all gather in one spot. Days that show her this is where she belongs. Sunday suppers was one way she reclaimed her old life, her normality. Seeing everything good she has in her life dulled that painful ache she carried so hard with her when she first came back to Nashville. She's where she's meant to be.

Sunday means family. Laughter. Love. Bad hangovers.

The soft ping of her phone on her nightstand takes her attention.

Propping herself up on her elbow, Sal checks her phone. There's a text from her sister, Lacey. *I got the Colin Cane account!!!*

She smiles, pride a buzz in her heart. She looks at Luke. "Lacey got that account she was working for."

"How many exclamation marks?" Luke drawls, a sly grin on his face.

"Three."

He gives her a look of sympathy. "Guess this means Nashville's out of the question."

Her smile fades. She had been trying to convince her sister to move to Nashville. The idea of Lacey out in LA all by herself wasn't her favorite. She wanted her closer, wanted to get to know her better. If there's one person who should be at their Sunday suppers, it's Lacey.

"Guess so."

"I'm sorry, darlin'," Luke says, running a hand down her arm. "I know how much you were itchin' to get her out here."

"It's okay," Sal says, turning an appreciative eye to her husband. The lean muscles in his back flex as he pulls himself into a sitting position. Chiseled shoulders. Those long, tan fingers she loves. "Can't win 'em all."

Yawning, Sal sits up, brushing dark hair over her shoulder. "What time is everyone coming over today?"

"The usual," Luke says. "Three. But Seth's headed over earlier to show me his new dirt bike."

"Which means in a month you'll have one of your own."

Luke laughs.

Shifting her position, Sal frowns. She sticks a hand between her legs. Her face must say it all because Luke's there. He moves to the side of her bed and sits down. His voice gentle, he says, "Why don't you take a shower and I'll change the sheets?"

Sal nods, refusing to let this ruin her day. Unfurling herself from the bed, she stands, only to be suddenly sideswiped by a wave of dizziness. The ground tilts under her. Spots strobe in front of her eyes.

"Hey." Firm hands grip her elbows, Luke's worried face appearing in front of her. She's lowered to sit on the edge of the bed. Luke kneels in front of her, still clasping her arm. "Sal, you okay?"

She shakes away wooziness. "I got lightheaded for a second there."

Luke's worried gaze tracks her.

Sal tilts her chin. "I'm fine, Luke."

He sighs. "If I had a damn penny . . ."

"Yeah, yeah, you'd be rich." She presses a kiss to his lips. Gives him a look. "Don't worry about me."

Luke stands, pulling her up with him. "Go shower."

Gripping his shoulder, Sal stands on tiptoes and kisses him hungrily. Her heart sparks, beats double time. A shiver runs through her as Luke caresses a hand along the arc of her spine.

Finally, they pull away. Sal grins. "You should come join me, country boy. Make sure I don't slip."

Luke's eyes flash, the smile spreading across his face feral and sly. With a wild hoot, he rushes her. Sal lets out a delighted giggle as he sweeps her into his arms and carries her into the bathroom.

The morning passes in a lazy haze and by the time Sal and Luke come downstairs, it's noon. She groans when she sees the kitchen. The wine bottle toppled like a bowling pin, the box of pizza with crusty crusts, the slumped afghan. Sal's pants. Her torn uniform top.

Luke raises a brow as if suddenly remembering last night. "Think we got carried away."

An amused laugh escapes her lips. "Oh, you think?" She heads straight for the coffeepot, flicking on the radio as she does so. "This requires coffee," she tells Luke.

Luke, in the process of sandwiching the wine bottle and Sal's top inside the pizza box, wiggles his eyebrows at her. "Or we skip the coffee and go back upstairs."

She laughs. "Rope it in, country boy."

Together, she and Luke work to tidy up the kitchen. He runs a quick mop around the room while Sal puts away the dishes, every so often stopping to pick up a button from her top. Soon there's a small pile of them on the counter. Finally, when the trash is bagged, the curtains open to let in the breeze, Luke pulls Sal into a quick two-step. He dances her around the kitchen, singing along with George Strait in a goofy old cowboy warble. He gives her a twirl, dips her down, and then Sal finds herself staring at the upside-down figure of Seth.

Her brother-in-law stands in the entrance of the kitchen, a hand hooked on his belt loops, a grin on his face, six-pack tucked against his side. "Coffee in the afternoon," he says, the deep rumble of his voice filling the airy space. "Must've been a late night."

Luke straightens Sal up. She's hit with a head rush as the blood rushes back to her face.

"You're one to talk," she says, crossing her arms as she takes in Seth's scruffy appearance. Black T-shirt, torn blue jeans, sandy blond hair standing on end.

Seth just laughs, stepping into the kitchen and setting the six-pack on the counter. He gives Sal a warm look and a big hug.

She hugs him back, just as hard.

In that second, their connection snaps taut. Familial, platonic. Better than a brother. A best friend. The second she met him, the second time, there was an instant camaraderie. A feeling of connection that's never left them. He's done so much for her and Luke; she doesn't know how they'd survive without him.

"What can I say?" Seth says, releasing Sal. "Really ripped up the town last night."

Looking past his brother, Luke lifts a brow. "Then where's the date?"

"She'll be right in."

Luke looks impressed. "Really?"

"Nah." Seth shrugs, gives a knowing grin. "Couldn't make it."

Luke snorts. "You ain't foolin' me. We both she never got an invite anyway." His eyes drift to the window, his jovial tone turning concerned. "I thought you said it was a dirt bike."

Sal joins Luke at the window. Seth's vintage Bronco is hooked up to a trailer that holds a brand-new sparkling ATV.

"Dirt bike, ATV, big difference," Seth drawls.

Luke's face, dark and serious, says there is, in fact, a big difference.

After a quick squeeze of Luke's arm, telling him to relax, Sal goes to the fridge, bringing out a bowl covered with tinfoil.

"Wait. You ain't cookin', are you?" Mock fear tinges Seth's voice.

Sal rolls her eyes.

She'll never escape it. She can't cook. Even her memory loss couldn't save her there. She once burned a lasagna so bad the neighbors a few farms over called the fire department. Hence the reason for potluck.

"I am gonna kick your ass," Sal says, and Seth dodges her shoulder punch to lift the lid on the bowl.

He breathes a sigh of relief. "Sangria."

"Sal worked hard on it," Luke says, his lips twitching. "Those oranges took her hours to cut up."

Sal narrows her eyes at the two of them. When they get together, they're the comedians of the century.

"Seth, the day you start bringing actual food to a potluck is the day you can start judging the shit I burn." She evaluates the six-pack and the sangria, the makeshift bar already stockpiled. She gives Luke a glance. "Let's hope the others bring food, or we'll be having a liquid dinner."

"How the good Lord intended it," Seth says with a wicked smile. He peers at her, his blue eyes evaluating. "Luke says you're workin' too much."

Luke scowls. "Smooth, Seth."

Sal fixes a look on her husband. "Oh, he does, does he?"

Without a word, Luke grabs the trash and makes for the back door.

Seth crosses his arms, watching her closely. "He's just worried about you. So am I."

"Uh-huh." Before Seth can get into it, she says, "You gonna get along with Griff today?"

"Nice subject change," Seth says, giving her a look that tells her she isn't getting out of it so easily. But he shrugs, his face taking on a scowl. "Sure, I'll get along with Griff. What kind of name is that anyway? Sounds like something you name a dog."

She smothers a smile. "It's just a name, Seth."

"Yeah, well, he's hangin' on Luke's heels like he's waiting for some kinda handout."

Sal doesn't know about that. She thinks Seth and Griff just don't get along. Seth, for good reason, ditched Griff on tour when she was found. Griff was pissed and had some choice things to say about Luke after the Alabama fiasco, which pissed Seth off to no end. But now, all's kosher between Luke and Griff, which means . . .

Sal cocks her head, a sudden thought occurring to her. "Wait. Are you jealous?"

Seth glowers. He's caught.

"You are." She slings a dishrag over her shoulder and smiles. "Aw, Seth, that's kinda cute."

"What's kinda cute?" The back door blows open, Luke striding inside.

"Sal and her jokes," Seth says smoothly. With a quick step, he's moving for the hallway, tossing Luke a look. "I'm headed out. You comin'?"

"Darlin' . . ."

Sal meets Luke's hangdog stare. He wants to play with cars with his brother.

She chuckles. "Go. I'll take care of the rest." She lifts a brow at the now clean kitchen. "Not like there's anything to take care of."

Luke kisses her, then there's the slam of the screen door.

The kitchen calm. For now.

She watches through the window, feeling an extra burst of contentedness, as Seth shows Luke his ATV. She should go for a run—she finally has some free time, no work, no touring—but her breasts ache and she feels extra exhausted. There's not much to do before everyone arrives for the BBQ, so she settles in to enjoy the quiet and her coffee. She texts Lacey back *Congratulations*, turns up the radio, dumps chips into a bowl.

The mundane. It feels so damn good.

She treasures this life. These memories she's made. She has over a year's worth. Memories she remembers. They are hers and no one can take them from her.

As she sits at the kitchen table, she reminds herself Luke's right. She wants a baby, but if it doesn't happen, she has Luke. Friends and family who love and care about her.

Second chances.

Soon, two ticks down to three, and then the first truck is cruising down the winding driveway that leads to the old farmhouse.

The slam of the screen door has Emmy Lou and Jace appearing. Luke follows with oil-stained hands, quickly grabbing a cooler from the pantry and toppling in the six-pack Seth had brought. Emmy Lou smiles, her platinum bob bouncing as she sashays into the kitchen with a platter of sweets in her hands. Dressed in a lilac-colored jumpsuit, a magnolia tucked behind her ear, she looks every inch the Georgia rodeo queen she is.

"Sweet tea with vodka," Jace says, setting a pitcher on the counter. The pile of alcohol grows. He shoots a quick glance at Luke. "That ATV's souped as shit."

"I know." Luke watches Seth closely through the window. "He's gonna drive too fast." Concern tinges his voice.

Sal brushes a hand across his arm. "You worry too much."

Luke grunts, his brow bunched. "Only about my family."

Sal knows he does. After nearly losing Seth to an

overdose ten years ago, Luke can't help slipping into over-protective big brother mode at times. He cares about Seth something fierce, and Sal knows he still fights the memory of finding Seth curled up in that bathtub. It haunts Luke. And even though the memory comes secondhand to Sal, it haunts her as well.

After a long glance at her husband, whose frown has finally eased, Sal turns to Emmy Lou. "Please tell me you brought food."

"Sure did, sugar," Emmy Lou trills. She arranges the platter on the counter and pulls back the cellophane to reveal cookies, tarts and chocolate truffles.

"Great, dessert." Sal floats Luke a panicked look. "We at least have meat?"

"Burgers and dogs." Luke steals a truffle from the tray. He hoots a laugh as he pops it in his mouth, dodging Emmy Lou's scolding swat. "Don't worry, darlin.'"

Jace grabs a beer from the cooler. He hands one to Luke and then leans over to crank up the radio. "Sal, your song's on."

Sal's lips part as Luke's croon fills the kitchen.

> Darlin, I'll protect you to the ends of the earth
> You can pick me up from my knees in the dirt
> And together, we'll both start over
> Walkin' that same ol' road on to forever.

"Roads," the number one song in the country, on the eponymous album, was the newest Brothers Kincaid song Luke had written for her after everything happened last year. Still, even now, she'll never stop loving the thrill she gets from catching Luke's song to her on the radio.

Emmy Lou surveys the stocked bar. "Well, if the boys

are helpin' themselves, should we start drinkin'?" Her eyes gleam as she reaches for a stack of red Solo cups and ladles out a generous helping of sangria.

Sal grins and grabs a cup. "Might as well."

Just as she's taking a sip, there's a loud rap and then the screen door's swinging open. Alabama Forester and Griff Greyson bustle in, guitars slung over their shoulders.

"It's hot as hell out there," Griff growls, wiping sweat off his brow.

Luke tosses him a beer. "This oughta fix it."

Griff catches it up, cracks it open, doing double duty as he sets the guitars in the hallway.

"Sorry we're late," Alabama says, juggling two heavy brown bags. Her face is flushed from the heat, her red hair bright as a stoplight against her stark white sundress.

Grinning, Sal goes to the couple, taking a bag to ease Alabama's load. "You're not late. You're right on time."

Griff curves a tattooed arm around Sal's shoulder. "How you doin', sweetheart?"

Sal smiles up at his scarred face. The tall, gruff cowboy cuts an intimidating figure, but Sal knows better. Against all odds, Griff and Alabama have become part of their country music family. Close, and not to mention damn loyal friends, despite all that happened with Luke and Mort.

"Doing perfect," Sal says. "How was the honeymoon?"

"Gorgeous," Alabama says.

Griff arcs a brow, his eyes on his wife. His lips curve in a wicked smile. "Tiring."

A snort from Jace.

Alabama rolls her eyes. "Good lord, Greyson. Please, spare them."

"You really need Jesus, Griff," Emmy Lou says, her prim feathers ruffled.

Griff chuckles, his job done.

"Would you like a drink?" Sal asks, doing her best to change the subject. "We have alcohol, alcohol and alcohol."

"Sweet tea," Alabama says.

"Do you want me to fire up the grill, darlin'?" Luke asks.

Sal sips her drink, feeling content, bright and buzzy. "Yes, please."

Luke drops a kiss to her temple, grabs the meat from the fridge. "Get the tongs, would you, Jace?"

Griff rubs his hands together, his eyes gleeful, ready to harass. "I wanna see this damn bike Seth's been talkin' about."

"ATV," Luke says unhappily.

"Got 'em, let's go," Jace says, snapping the tongs together, and he and Griff follow Luke out.

Alabama adds the food she's brought to the buffet line. "Oh, thank god," Sal says. She lifts the lid on the Styrofoam containers only to be hit with a waft of delicious scents. Cornbread biscuits, collard greens, macaroni and cheese, potato salad. "You brought sides."

Alabama flushes. "We got 'em from the deli. Lord, I probably bought up the whole store. I'm sorry. We've been so busy with the honeymoon and the album." Her gray eyes light up. "And we're buyin' a house."

Sal pours herself a second cup of sangria and hops up, sitting on the counter. "Really? Congrats, Al. That's great."

"How excitin'," Emmy Lou drawls. "Where?"

Sal notes the smile on Emmy Lou's face. Honest.

Pleasant. Emmy Lou's been slow to warm up to Alabama after everything that's happened, but she's gotten there.

"East Nashville," Alabama says. "It's an older place, a fixer-upper. I just can't wait to get my hands on it." She lifts her eyes to the kitchen, taking in the beams and the crown molding, then blushes. "Though heaven knows when we'll get around to it."

Emmy Lou laughs. "Sounds like y'all are still in the honeymoon phase."

Sal, lifting the glass to her lips, says, "Honeymoon's the best part."

"If that ain't the truth." Emmy Lou smiles, but her voice has taken on a sad tone.

"I imagine y'all still in it?" Alabama smiles, taking Sal's attention away from Emmy Lou. "You and Luke."

She blushes, thinking of the underwear she picked up off of the pendant light this afternoon. "We may or may not have our moments."

At that, as if Luke's been waiting for the perfect time to underscore her words, a fireball goes up in the backyard with a great *whoosh*.

Alabama hisses under her breath, swearing.

Emmy Lou squeals.

Sal drops the cup from her lips. She can practically feel the heat on her face from the grill. Hear Seth's maniacal laughter from the backyard. Smoke curls beneath a window. "Jesus."

Alabama's lips twitch. "Think we need to go oversee this so they don't burn the place down?"

"Good idea." Sal slips off the counter, only to find that

the lightheadedness is back. She palms the counter to catch herself and exhales.

Alabama looks at her. "All okay?"

Sal laughs. "That's some strong sangria."

"C'mon, sugar." Emmy Lou links arms with Sal and the women slip out the back door.

chapter
FOUR

THE SUN BEATS HOT AGAINST THE BACKYARD, THE sparkle of the river in the distance, the soft sway of wildflowers in the breeze. Luke throws open the double doors of the formal dining room and looks around for the beer he misplaced. Seth comes in with a bottle of wine, while Emmy Lou, Jace, Griff and Alabama stand on the deck in animated conversation. By now, there's a small village of people in their home. The long wooden table seats twelve, but Sal sets it for nine.

She surveys the room, smiling in utter happiness. She loves the chaos, the bickering, the bullshitting. The only thing she'd add to it would be—

Stop, she thinks to herself. *Stop thinking about babies.*

She thought she had steadied herself after her talk with Luke, but it keeps poking its damn head in her thoughts.

Luke stands, arms crossed. A frown on his handsome face. "I've lost two damn beers since we started."

"That's your goddamn right at a BBQ," Seth cackles. He appears beside Sal, pouring her a glass of wine.

"You're a terrible enabler," Sal says to Seth's mischievous grin. She points to the mantel. "Your beer, Luke."

He tosses her a wink and grabs it up.

"I'll get the food," Sal says.

"Here, I'll help you," Alabama offers, coming up alongside Sal and following her down the hallway.

Inside the kitchen, Sal arranges cornbread on a platter while Alabama grabs condiments from the fridge. Sal's stomach burbles in hunger, the scent of honey butter and macaroni and cheese scenting the kitchen. She blinks, realizing she hasn't eaten a thing today. Besides the coffee. The sangria. The wine. Liquid lunch is right.

Alabama leans back against the counter. "I didn't want to say anything with Emmy Lou there, but how are you doin'? With everything?" Her words are loaded and Sal understands what she's asking.

Besides Lacey, Sal's confided in Alabama about the fact that she and Luke were having a hard time trying for a baby. Though the tabloids, including the *Star*—especially the *Star*—doubt their friendship, claiming it was to garner sympathy for Alabama or to sell records for the Brothers Kincaid, Sal knows the truth. She and Alabama are friends. And only they know the real story.

Sal takes a great gulp of her wine and shrugs. "The same."

Alabama winces. "Ugh. I'm so sorry, Sal."

"Don't be." Sal grabs the pitcher of iced tea and the bowl of mac and cheese. "I appreciate you asking."

A bright blast of music fills the house, the crackle of the record player signaling Luke means business. Soon, it'll be dinner, then more whiskey, then guitars around the bonfire.

Food in their hands, Sal and Alabama exit the kitchen, taking a left down the hall to the dining room. At their appearance, Seth barrels toward her, taking the heavy jug of iced tea from her hands. Seeing Sal, Luke whistles to get the attention of the buzzed group on the porch.

"Like wranglin' cats," Alabama drawls as Griff steps inside, raising his aviators.

Everyone gathers, Luke taking his seat at the head of the table, Sal to his left. Beside Sal, Griff, then Alabama. Across the table, Seth, Emmy Lou, Jace. In silence, everyone digs in, filling their plates, lifting heavy platters, passing bowls. Emmy Lou nudges Seth for the bottle of wine, giggling as he pretends to fight her for it.

Sal looks around the table, soaking up the strange sense of normalcy of being homebound for a few months before everyone goes back on tour again.

"How was the gig in Shreveport?" Luke asks, pointing to Griff with his beer. "Heard you barely made it out of there in one piece."

Griff glowers, spearing a hunk of mac and cheese. "Fuckin' press. They cut the tour bus off tryin' to get a damn picture. Nearly ran us off the road."

"What do you expect?" Jace says. "Gotta get their picture, blood or bust."

"Played a whole lick on my guitar, so it wasn't a total loss," Alabama adds, lifting her wine glass to her lips.

Luke's eyes widen. "No shit."

Sal grins, leaning back in her chair to look at Alabama. "Good for you."

To Griff, Luke says, "We're workin' on a song with you next week, ain't we?"

"Lookin' forward to it, Kincaid." Griff cuts a look at Luke, his lips twitching in amusement. "Although, I don't know if y'all need the competition. With me there, the Brothers Kincaid might be on their way out."

Luke chuckles. "Fuck you."

Sal hides a smirk as Seth rolls his eyes.

"Okay, I say this lovingly, but it is the weekend and y'all are clowns because I know we are not talkin' about work right now," Emmy Lou says, her eyes narrowed with annoyance.

Jace lifts a fork stacked with potato salad to his lips. "I don't think that's how it works, Em."

"Sure, we'll change the subject," Griff says easily. "Let's talk about Seth's new ride." He shakes his head in disgust. "Fuckin' shame. That paint color."

Seth wraps a hand around his beer. "Hey, leave ol' June out of this."

Emmy Lou props an elbow on the table, looks at Seth with a smile. "Oh, she has a name now?"

Sal laughs and sips her wine. "It's the new lady in his life. We have to accept her."

Luke meets Sal's eyes, laughter dancing on his face. They both know Seth's girlfriends are short-lived and scarce.

"Oh, Seth?" Jace snorts. "I don't think his heart has ever skipped a beat in his life."

Griff leans in, leveling Seth with a look. "You off-road anything more than forty-five degrees, you're gonna roll it, you know that, don't you?"

Luke tenses in his chair at the words.

Seth tosses his fork down, a scowl on his usually sunny face. "What is this, pick on Seth hour?"

Griff shrugs. "When you got a shitty ride, sure."

"Yeah, well, you know what? You got a shitty fuckin'

attitude, Greyson," Seth snaps. "Nothin' much has changed since we left your ass in Florida. Luke might throw you a few bones with a song, but you're still an asshole."

Silence falls across the table.

Sal bites her lip, too stunned by the outburst to say anything. Emmy Lou, her light brown eyes wide, gives Sal a stare that says *too much alcohol.*

Griff growls, anger on his face, a hot retort on his lips, but Alabama lays a hand on his arm. "Griff."

A calm comes over him, a calm only Alabama can bring out, and he settles back in his chair, disgruntled, twisting a gold ring on his pinkie.

Sal glances around the table. Emmy Lou, in the middle of sawing her burger in half, is wincing, Jace frowning, and Luke. . .

Luke's giving his brother a sharp look, silently warning him not to continue this path of conversation. A moment passes between the two of them and then Seth's dark glare clears.

Seth digs up a massive helping of potato salad, grumbles, "Guy can't take a damn joke." As close to an apology as he can get.

Emmy Lou waves a hand around the table like she can scoop up everyone and shake them out into a different mood. "I take it back, I think y'all should go back to talkin' work," she chirps, ever the bright light amidst Seth's sullen scowl.

Griff busts out with an ear-splitting laugh that shakes the house, even Seth joins in on the laughter as the table returns to more lighthearted conversation.

Only Sal shifts uncomfortably. The record player

suddenly seems so loud. The house too hot. It feels as if her head might float away from her body. Then, feeling eyes on her, she looks over at Luke and gives him a smile, not wanting him to worry. As the howling laughter swells around her, she closes her eyes and breathes a shaky breath in.

Luke studies Sal, her cheeks pink from the heat. Her bright green eyes stare off into space, her face distracted. Deciding that Seth and Griff won't full-on beat each other's ass, he turns his attention to her. "You okay?" he whispers, leaning in.

She nods. Her smile forced. Luke fights a frown, studying her plate. She hasn't touched her food. Hasn't said much of anything really.

He looks away from Sal as Jace laughs, turning the conversation to lighter things like rodeos and record deals.

"Sal?" Seth's frowning across the table.

"I'm okay," she says.

And then she faints in her chair.

She lists left, but Griff's quick, catching her up before she can fall out of her chair and hit the ground. "Fuck," he breathes, staring down in dismay at an unconscious Sal in his arms.

For a heartbeat, the entire table sits frozen, and then it erupts.

Luke rips his chair back.

Seth rockets up. The table is jarred as everyone lurches to standing. Chairs screech as they're roughly shoved away.

"Oh my god!" Emmy Lou cries out, gripping Jace's shoulder.

Griff, cradling Sal tightly against his chest, passes her to Luke and together they lower her gently to the ground.

Alabama places a hand over her heart, watching with worried eyes.

Everything moves in slow motion. Voices, questions swarm the air around them.

"Is she okay?"

"Did she choke on something?"

"Is it a migraine?"

"Should I get her medication?"

"I don't know, I don't know," Luke says. He doesn't know anything except the fact that his wife's out cold and his heart's in his goddamn throat. Hovering over Sal, he frantically feels for a pulse. Her heartbeat thumps strong beneath his fingers. Letting out a relieved breath, he cups the side of her face. "Sal, darlin', wake up."

Griff kneels beside Sal, resting a broad hand across the top of her dark head. He's had a soft spot for Sal ever since she stepped in and saved Alabama when she was shot taking a bullet meant for Griff. He looks to Luke, his brow drawn in concern. "What do we do, Kincaid?"

"Somethin' cool," Luke says tersely. "For her face."

Emmy Lou runs for the kitchen.

"Fuck," Seth says, covering his mouth with his palm. "Fuck."

It's chaos, commotion, and all Luke can do is worry about Sal. His entire body's on life support. He needs the green of her eyes, her smile, her voice to keep breathing.

"C'mon, Sal," he says, patting her hard on the cheeks in an effort to rouse her. "Wake up, darlin'. Come back to me."

There's motion above Luke. Emmy Lou hurrying back with a cool washrag, passing it down to Griff, who presses it against Sal's temple.

No response. Still no response.

Fear grabs Luke by the throat. "Sal!" His voice rises, urgent, panicked. "Sal, you gotta wake up." His hands tremble as he cups her cheek, her face lolling in his palm.

Christ, please, he thinks desperately. *Don't let something be wrong. Her head. Her memory. Her health.*

Jace's urgent voice floats above. "She ain't wakin' up, Luke."

"Lord, what do we do?" Alabama asks.

A harsh exhale blasts from Seth. He's pacing a hole in the floor. "She's been out, Luke. Too long."

Griff, his tawny eyes on Sal's expressionless face, looks to Luke. In a low voice, he says, "Kincaid, maybe we oughta—"

But Luke's already ahead of him. He's hooking one arm beneath the small of her back, the other under her neck, prepared to haul ass to the hospital when Sal moans.

"Oh, thank Christ," he breathes. He stares, his throat so tight, air can't get past. He watches as Sal's eyes flutter, then slowly open. The green of her eyes his salvation.

Griff smiles down at Sal. "Welcome back, sweetheart."

Sal's eyes are glassy with confusion as she blinks, takes in the crowd above her. Her beautiful face pulls into a frown. "Luke, what . . . ?"

Before she can say another word, she's in Luke's arms and he's standing. He looks over his shoulder as he exits the dining room, the concerned eyes of his friends and family on him.

"What do you need us to do?" Jace asks, wrapping an arm around Emmy Lou.

"Eat." He says it only because he knows Sal would want them to. "I'm gonna get her upstairs."

As he turns for the hallway, he catches a glimpse of his brother's worried face. "C'mon," he hears Seth order reluctantly. "You heard Luke. Let's sit the fuck back down."

Upstairs, Luke settles Sal on the bed. She blinks, the cloudiness leaving her eyes as she comes fully back to consciousness. "What happened?"

He sits beside her, smoothing a lock of hair from her cool forehead. "You fainted, darlin.'"

Sal's eyes, her mouth fly open. "Oh god." She groans in embarrassment, burying her face in her palms. "No one's ever gonna come to our house again."

Luke's too worried to laugh. He peers at her, taking her in with shrewd eyes. Her pallor moon-white. Purple bruises beneath her eyes. "Stay here," he says, giving her a look that means business.

Shoving off the bed, he goes to the bathroom. He finds her migraine medication in the medicine cabinet, only when he returns to the bedroom, he's greeted by Sal shaking her head.

"No," she says. "It's not a migraine. My head's fine. . ."

He sits beside her. "Then what is it?"

"I don't know." Her eyes narrow as she searches her

mind. "When we sat down, I started to feel off. Really warm. Lightheaded."

"How are you feelin' now?"

A tilt of her dark head, as if she's evaluating her current condition. "I feel fine now. Really."

A flare of frustrated worry hits him as he stares at his wife. "You sure as hell ain't fine, Sal." He takes her hand, needing the contact. The feel of her, that she's here and present. "Passin' out at the dinner table ain't okay. Something's wrong."

Sal's lips thin out. "Luke."

He shakes his head. He's winning this argument. While he appreciates Sal's stubbornness, she ain't talking herself out of this. Not tonight, not after what happened back in the dining room.

"Darlin', you're workin' double shifts. Runnin' yourself ragged. Worryin' about everyone but yourself. You're gonna make yourself sick and I ain't havin' that."

As proud as he is of Sal getting her job back as quick as she has, it also concerns him. He knows she's thrown herself into her job, especially after they lost the two pregnancies. And it's as much his fault as hers. Hell, he's been dragging her on the road, touring too damn much when he should be thinking of her. It's only been a year since he got her back. Only six months since her migraines, the nightmares stopped. He should have been paying closer attention. Damn him.

"I'm sorry," he says to Sal, whose expression has gone shamefaced and sad. "I'm not angry, I'm worried. I'm worried about you, Sal." He squeezes her hand. "Your mom had health issues. I don't want you to wait until it's too late."

Inhaling deep, Sal closes her eyes at the mention of a mother she still cannot remember.

"Okay." Her eyes open, resolute. "You're right. I'll get checked out when I go back to work Tuesday. I'll ask Tawny to run a panel."

"Thank you." He leans in, sweeping dark hair from her face, some of his worry dissolving at the thought of getting an answer. "You let me know the time, I'll be there. I'll cancel—"

"No." She shifts on the pillows, curling up into a small ball. Her hands beneath her cheek, she stares up at Luke. "You do the interview."

Luke's jaw tightens. He wants to tell her that her health's more important than the damn interview, but he bites his tongue.

"Besides," she says, "it'll be fine. I'll be fine."

But he doesn't miss the tremble in her voice that tells him she's scared.

He leans down to kiss her, battling worry and doubt. "I want you to rest," he says, laying a palm against the curve of her hip. Sal doesn't answer. She just closes her eyes, a tear slipping down her cheek.

Luke sits with Sal until she falls asleep. Downstairs, he can hear people scurrying around, cleaning up as quietly as possible. Gently, he slips Sal's hand into his. The pulse in her wrist beats strong and healthy, but still, the fear that's slowly dissipated over the last year bubbles up from its depths.

She has to be okay. She has to.

Downstairs, Luke finds the kitchen cleaned up and the house cleared out. When he steps onto the back porch, he sees Seth, staring into the dark. A bottle of bourbon balances on the porch railing. Hearing Luke, the crack of the door, Seth straightens up and turns. "She okay?"

"She's restin.'"

Relief passes between the brothers, a calming of adrenaline, of nerves.

"Thank Christ," Seth exhales. "Think I had 'bout five years scared off my life."

"You're tellin' me." Luke joins Seth at the railing, surveying the empty driveway. "Thanks for cleanin' up."

Seth nods. "No problem. Em did most of the work." He passes his brother a glass of honey-colored liquid, which Luke promptly shoots back. Seth stares at him a long moment before refilling it.

Luke sits in a chair and buries his face in his hands. He breathes in and out. He wants to punch a door. Punch something. Hard. He feels helpless. So goddamn helpless.

Seth's low rumble shakes up the night. "Luke, you okay?"

"I don't know." Luke's voice is thick with grief. "I don't know what the hell's goin' on. She's goin' to see a doctor Tuesday. If something's wrong . . ." He breaks off, stricken. His chest aches like a bitch, like his heart's being torn apart.

Seth drops into a chair beside him. "Nothing's wrong with Sal. You hear me? You're worryin' about something that hasn't happened yet."

Luke's throat knots. He's so damn grateful for his brother. For continuously being a silent source of comfort, for always having his back. For looking after Sal. He doesn't know what he'd do without Seth. His brother's been there for him through the lowest lows and highest highs, and Luke intends to do the same. Whenever Seth needs it.

Luke smears a hand down his face, drains his bourbon. "The baby stuff's too much." He shakes his head, lost in thought, almost talking to himself. "It was too soon. We should have waited longer. I don't know what it'll do to her if we lose any more."

Seth's brow furrows. "Any more?"

"We lost a few," he grits out, the admission painful. While Seth knows they're trying, Luke's spared him all the gory details. "After Henry. One late last year. One a few months ago."

"Shit, man." Seth's wincing. "I'm sorry."

"It's hard to take. Seein' her in pain." His throat knots up and he damn near chokes on the words. "I want to help her, but I can't. I can't fix it. I can't do fuckin' anything."

Sympathy clouds Seth's eyes. He leans over to clasp his brother on the shoulder. "You're doin' your best, Luke. You can't protect her from everything. Even though I know you want to. Hell, even though *I* want to."

Luke nods, his jaw tight as he battles his demons. Battles his worry that the world they've been living in so safely for the last year could be easily shattered at any time.

"How are you doin' with it?" Seth asks. "It can't be easy on you either."

He meets his brother's stare. Telling him he's worried. Telling him he cares. With a shaky exhale, Luke bows his head and grips the back of his neck. "Christ," he says, and his voice is a rain cloud beginning to leak. "It's hard to take. I can't take anything else. I can't lose anything more."

Seth squeezes Luke's shoulder. Together, they sit in silence, the night opening around them, the chirr of crickets, the soft neigh of the ponies in the field, fireflies blinking their golden light.

Somewhere in the house, a floorboard creaks. Seth glances over his shoulder at the screen door, frowns, then turns back to Luke. "It's all gonna work out, man."

Luke nods, sucks in a breath as he stares out into the dark. "Yeah. I hope so."

chapter
FIVE

S AL SITS ON THE EXAM ROOM TABLE, HER LEG bouncing a mile a minute. Five vials of blood drawn. She needs to lie down. Or better yet, have a drink.

She closes her eyes, her mind automatically going to her botched Sunday supper. Worse, what she overheard that night. She had been coming downstairs to find Luke but instead found him and Seth. Luke's worry practically burned a hole in the screen door. His pained words to his brother: *I can't take anything else.* She retreated before they could spot her, but Luke's distraught words have haunted her for the last two days.

It's taking a toll not only on her, but on Luke too. She hadn't realized just how much. He's been trying to be so strong for her, while hiding his own pain.

Well, no more.

She can't do this to him. To them. She has to give this up. She has to be strong for Luke and let whatever will be, be.

The sound of the door opening has Sal looking up. Tawny steps into the room, carrying Sal's chart.

It's Tuesday night, their shift over. Her friend offered to stay with her while Nurse Buntin ran a panel.

"Well?" Sal rubs her sweaty palms on her jeans. "What's the verdict?"

A strange smile grows on Tawny's face. "You ready for this? You're pregnant."

Sal's jaw drops. "What?"

"Yep. Got the results from Buntin right here."

"But, but . . ." Sal's world whirls. "I'm on my period."

Her brain tries to make sense of it, her legs, her mind Jell-O. She's had her period the last two months. Lighter than usual, but she's still had it.

"Not a period," Tawny says. "Implantation bleeding. Some women have it their whole pregnancy."

Sal shakes her head, sets her mouth in a hard line. "Run it again."

"Sal."

"Run it again, Tawny."

Tawny settles beside Sal at the exam table, her eyes sympathetic, yet tinged with humor. "Look, I knew you'd say that and I did. I ran it twice. You're officially, definitely pregnant." She pokes a finger at Sal's chart. "The fainting was probably caused by anemia, because you're low on iron. And you need to drink more water because you're dehydrated as fuck."

Sal shakes her head, disbelief, worry, sideswiping joy. "There's something wrong. There's no morning sickness, no—"

"Sal," Tawny soothes. "A lot of women don't have morning sickness. That's doesn't mean something's wrong."

Her heart aches to hope.

For a long minute, Sal sits stunned, touching her fingertips to her lips. Then out of her mouth comes a tear-filled laugh. "Oh my god. I don't believe it."

"Well, believe it, sweetcheeks." Tawny nudges her shoulder. "Let's go up to obstetrical and see McKibbon. She owes me a favor."

"Ten weeks?" Sal asks, shocked. She sits up on her elbows, turning her eyes to the screen.

Dr. McKibbon runs the ultrasound wand across Sal's stomach. "Looks like it."

Sal's eyes fill with tears at the sight of her beautiful blur of baby. She can make out the head, what will be feet, hands. And the heartbeat. It's steady. Strong. It's really there. A baby.

Her and Luke's baby.

Dr. McKibbon presses deeper on her stomach with the wand. "So, that would put the date of conception right around June fifteenth."

Sal chokes on a laugh. She'd never forget that date. Alabama and Griff's wedding reception. It was held at a 125-acre ranch outside Nashville. She and Luke had been having a grand old time, enjoying a night off from everything, and then two beers turned into five, and before Sal knew it, they were sneaking off to the upstairs bathroom, Luke lifting her up on the sink, his big hands running warm over her body, Sal hiking up her dress.

"Right now," McKibbon's calm voice sideswipes Sal's memory, "it looks like a healthy baby."

Sal turns her head to her. "What about the spotting?"

"It should stop," says McKibbon. "It's rare, and terrifying, but some women do spot their entire pregnancy. It's not always a sign that something is wrong. I understand why you'd be more worried than usual, but everything looks good, Sal." McKibbon smiles and powers down the machine. "Congratulations."

She inhales deeply and nods. "Thank you."

As Dr. McKibbon exits the room, Sal slowly sits up on the exam table, dazed yet euphoric. Still, she stays seated on the exam table. She doesn't trust her legs.

A quick knock sounds on the door and then Tawny's popping her head into the room. "How'd it go?"

Sal's mouth works the words over. "Everything's okay. I'm ten weeks."

Tawny laughs, giving her a hug. "Hot damn. You want me to call Luke?"

It's automatic. "No," she says, snagging Tawny's arm.

Tawny arcs a brow. She's already pegged her thoughts. "Sal, you can't keep it from him."

"Only until I'm twelve weeks." She gives Tawny a pleading look. "I've never made it this far before. I don't want to get his hopes up. I just want to be sure."

"Whatever you think." Tawny sighs. "You know what's best." She pats Sal's hand. "I'm so happy for you, Sal. I'll let you get dressed."

Sal covers her face and laughs into her palms as a burst of happiness so huge crashes into her heart. Holy shit, she's pregnant. It's a dream. A miracle. A damn out-of-the-blue present from the universe.

Less than a week ago, she and Luke were bemoaning

the fact that they couldn't get pregnant. And now, everything's suddenly rearranged in her world. Her palms drift from her face to cup her stomach. She has to keep this close. Safe. Quiet. It's just for two weeks, until the risk of miscarriage is lower. She needs to do this for Luke. For the last year, he's been her rock. Always making sure she knew she was loved. Gentle with her memory and kind with her heart. Putting her first, protecting her.

Now, it's her turn to protect him.

After several deep breaths, Sal slides off the exam table, dresses, and exits the room. She's walking down the hall in a happy haze when there's a hand on her elbow. Sal stops in her tracks. She blinks at the girl in front of her. "Molly."

The girl bites her lip. "I'm sorry, I didn't know where else to go."

"Don't be sorry," Sal says. "C'mere." She leads the girl to an empty lounge. "What's going on?" She keeps her voice even and calm even though it's clear as day what's going on. Molly's got a black eye, a busted lip as big as Texas.

"I need help. And you said—"

"Yes." Sal nods, her heart beating out a relieved beat. That this girl is asking for help. That she left before it was too late. Sal's been there. She's done it. She knows how hard it is. "The Mary Parrish Center is a shelter. They'll help you and your baby."

Molly shrinks back against the wall. "He'll find me."

Sal shakes her head. "He won't. I promise you."

Molly's brown eyes dart down the hall, then back to Sal. "I need to go home and get my things—"

"No." Sal's voice is sharp. Adamant. "No, you don't." She digs into her pockets and pulls out the cash she keeps on her for lunches and coffee runs. It's not much, but it'll get the girl a toothbrush, a change of clothes. She presses it into Molly's palms. "Take this, okay? Get yourself what you need and then go straight to the shelter."

Tears well in Molly's eyes. She grips the cash and Sal's hand. "Thank you so much."

"Go," Sal urges.

After a long glance at Sal, Molly lets go of her hand and exits the lounge.

Sal stands there for a long while, covering her stomach protectively with her palms, and then closes her eyes.

Lucky.

She's damn lucky.

chapter SIX

W HEN SAL GETS HOME A LITTLE AFTER SIX, Luke's already there, waiting for her. He's raising a brow, straightening up from his perch on the front porch step. "Well?" he asks, coming toward her to meet her in the gravel drive. Taking her gently by the shoulders, he peers into her face. "What's the word, darlin'?"

Love ripples through her. Luke's been worrying all day. She'll never stop loving how he cares so damn much, how he'll do anything necessary to take care of her.

She reaches up and grips his thin black tie. He's still in the suit from his photoshoot. "Well, word is, your girl's anemic."

Relief flashes across his face. "That's it?"

"With a side of dehydration."

He groans, rolling his eyes up to the pink sky. "Sal . . ."

"I know," she says quickly, intercepting his worry. She smiles. "I'm okay, though, I promise."

"You sure?"

"So sure. Don't worry."

"I always worry."

"Just kiss me, Luke." Taking his handsome face between her hands, Sal stands on tiptoes to kiss him deeply. She tastes the whiskey on his breath, the scent of rosewood oil and wood shavings.

Luke responds by wrapping his arms around her waist to pull her closer. His kiss—tender, sparking—has her blood pulsing, her heart beating as if it will never stop.

When they break away, gasping, chuckling, Luke's lean hands cup her cheek. He stares at her, nothing but love in his warm, dark eyes.

She damn near melts right then and there. She's so tempted. Tempted to tell Luke. It's on the tip of her tongue. She's pregnant. A new road. A baby.

But the anticipation, the excitement's quickly chased away. It hits her like a brick. She could lose it. Again. Another baby gone.

She tunes out the awful thought. Tunes out the guilt about keeping her news from Luke. Instead, she reminds herself about the conversation she overheard on Sunday.

It's only for two weeks. She'll hit twelve weeks and tell him then.

Until then, she can't get his hopes up.

She turns her cheek into his palm, savoring his touch. Looking up at him through heavy lashes, she asks, "How was the interview?"

He scoffs, his drawl tight and irritated. "They had us out in a cornfield in damn suits. Hot as hell, sweating for two hours."

"Bet they got some good photos." Sal eyes Luke with appreciation. He looks sharp and sexy in the dark navy suit.

"They better have or Seth will never let me hear the

end of it." He chuckles. "Interview was good, though. It'll be great for the album. How about you?"

She nuzzles against his broad chest, letting the warmth, the strength of his body support her. "It's been a weird day." The closest to the truth she can get. She smiles. "But a good one."

Luke traces a finger across her cheekbone. His eyes search out hers. "Yeah?"

"Yeah." Sal kisses him again and whispers, "A great one."

Luke frowns. Every light in the kitchen is off.

Dark. Dim. Silence.

Sal stands near the fridge, her dark hair cascading over her shoulders, her eyes blank. She stares at Luke. She holds out her hand.

In it, a miniature airplane.

Luke blinks in confusion. "Sal . . ."

He tries to move toward her but can't. He's held tight by a seat belt strapped across his waist. He fights to unbuckle it.

He watches in horror as, from behind Sal, a meaty arm wraps around her stomach. Claiming. Taunting.

"No!" Luke strains against his bindings. His heart threatens to beat itself out of his chest.

A rasp comes from Roy's mouth. "I'll take her again."

Sal closes her eyes, leaning back against Roy. "Luke." Her words are stricken, fading. She's fading. Her body getting faint, dissipating into a mist.

He opens his mouth to yell, to shout her name, but she's gone. He blinks and Sal's gone. But he can hear her.

Her heartbeat, her scream in his ears, her hands reaching for—

Luke wakes in a cold sweat, jolting up in bed with a gasp. He wrenches left, immediately seeking out Sal. The ache in his gut uncoils as his eyes land on his wife. He lets out a breath of relief at the sight of her sleeping easy beside him, curled up against him in a loose ball.

Luke closes his eyes, willing his heartbeat to come down. His breath to even out. Sal's here. Beside him. Her chest rising and falling evenly. Looking like a damn goddess in her white nightgown, her dark hair unbound around her. So why can't he shake the thought that something's wrong?

He exhales, shaky. These goddamn nightmares.

He had thought that after Sal returned, after he got back into his music, the dreams of her and the plane crash would go away. But they only morphed into something different. Something darker. Roy. Taking Sal. He can't help but clench a fist at the thought. That motherfucker.

Luke buries his face in his hands. "Fuck."

A rustle of movement beside him.

Beside him, Sal's opening her eyes, pushing herself up on an elbow. On alert, as if she's been waiting to comfort him. "Luke?"

"It's okay, darlin'," he says softly, hating himself that he woke her. She's got an early shift and needs her sleep.

She frowns. "No. It's not okay." She eases herself up in bed and scoots close. She touches his cheek, moving his face toward hers. Her eyes are searching, sorrowful. "Another nightmare?"

"Yeah. But don't worry about it." He leans in and kisses

the curve of her shoulder. "You got work tomorrow. I'm sorry I woke you. Go back to bed."

Her full lips thin out, that adorable look on her face she gets when she's frustrated with him. She brushes a lock of hair from his head. "Don't ever be sorry about that, Luke." She makes a face, her green eyes shining with understanding. "Was it very bad?"

He gives her a grin. "Ain't nothin' I can't handle."

She takes one look at his face and shakes her head. "Liar."

He pulls her against him. Sal lets out a sweet sigh as she nestles into his arms, and together they lie back against the pillows. Tucking Sal's small frame against his side, Luke closes his eyes in relief. Reminds himself the news from the doctor was positive.

She's healthy. She's fine.

Safe.

With him.

His gaze drifts to Sal. Her sleepy eyes stare back at him, her expression content, serene. Drop-dead gorgeous. "I love you, darlin'," he says, brushing his lips against her temple.

Her lips part, her smile like a light in the dark. "I love you always, Luke Kincaid."

Luke pulls her in tighter. Love. It's always been love with Sal and nothing else. Nothing better. All he needs.

chapter

SEVEN

SAL'S BRIGHT YELLOW RUNNING SHOES FLY across soft earth. Loam and pine needles spray up behind her as she races back to the house. The afternoon sun burns bright in the noon-blue sky.

She needed this run, needed a way to decompress before her night shift at the hospital.

It's been a week of lying low, of drinking enough water and going to sleep early and taking pregnancy tests every damn day to soothe her nerves. She's never been so tired in her entire life. But then, she's never been so grateful.

It's still there, she tells herself. That little baby deep and safe in her belly.

Sal slows her stride when she makes it back to the farm. She pounds up the stairs right into the house. For the first time in a long time, it's empty. She takes in the strange silence. No one is playing music, the radio going at eardrum-bursting decibels, Seth and Luke arguing about the most pointless things only they can argue about. Only an odd quiet. Stillness.

Sal prefers the noise. It means life is happening. Her life.

At the kitchen sink, she fills a glass with water. She drinks fast, gulps. She knows she's dehydrated, can fill the lightheadedness creeping over her, the cramp in her side a pinch.

Sal catches a glimpse of her reflection in the window pane, her breath held heavy in her chest. She's going to be a mother. Hell, she was a mother. She can't remember her Henry, but she knows she loved him more than anything.

And Luke. Sal smiles, her heart giddy. He'll be the best father.

Setting the glass down, Sal goes to step away from the sink, only to be swept up by a wave of dizziness. It happens sudden and fast. She tries to grab the kitchen counter but misses.

Shit, not again, she thinks.

She braces herself for the fall, but instead, a strong arm wraps around her waist. Holding her up. Tight.

"I got you."

A rumble of a voice.

Seth. He's here. At her side. She hadn't heard him come in. Hadn't heard much of anything as her ears emptied of sound and her world blurred.

Sal lets Seth lead her to the living room, settling her gently on the couch. The cushion shifts as he sits beside her. Then Sal's world refocuses. She blinks up at Seth. He's leaning in, his blue eyes cloudy with worry.

She sweeps hair from her face. "What're you doing here?"

"I came over to return Luke's tools." He gestures at the rusted toolbox sitting in the foyer. "And a good thing too because I almost found you on the floor."

She opens her mouth to protest, when the world around her swirls. Dizzy, she squeezes her eyes shut and waits for her vision to clear.

"That's it." A crack in Seth's voice. "I'm callin' Luke."

"No." She peels her eyes open, resting a hand on Seth's forearm before he can pull out his phone. "Please."

He hits her with a hard look that tells her he won't buy her bullshit any longer. "What's goin' on, Sal? Luke said you went to the doctor."

"I did."

"And he said everything was okay."

She bites her lip, debating what to say. "I kinda, maybe kept something from him . . ."

Seth scrubs a hand down his face. "Are you sick?" When she's silent, he exhales roughly. His voice rises—not mad, but worried—as he says, "Goddamnit, Sal."

"I'm not sick, I'm pregnant."

The words hit Seth like a truck and he starts. Then his eyes clear, his expression changing from agony to relief. "Sal, goddamn, that's great." He crushes her in a big hug that takes the air from her lungs. When he pulls back, his blue eyes are wide and wet. "Luke's gotta be thrilled."

"He doesn't know yet." Seth's brow furrows and before he can ask, she blurts, "And you can't tell him."

He sighs.

"Please."

"No way."

"Please, Seth."

"But why?" he asks, mystified. "Luke, he's gonna be so goddamned happy. You gotta know that. "

She inhales shakily. "I know that. I do. It's just so early." Hot tears fill her eyes. "I don't want to get his hopes up again."

Seth leans back and evaluates her. "So you're what? Gonna tell him when the baby's five?"

She laughs, loving Seth. Only he can make her laugh when she feels close to breaking.

Seth continues, shaking his head. "I don't know, Sal. What about you? You're doin' this alone."

"No, I'm not. I have you."

He rolls his eyes. "Great."

"I know it's a lot to ask to hide it from Luke, but I have to be sure. Just one more week and then I'll tell him." The minute she says it, she's hit by a rush of excitement. To tell Luke. Lacey. Everyone in their family.

Seth rips a hand through his sandy-blond hair. "Fine. I don't like keepin' things from Luke, but I also really fuckin' hate that look on your face."

Her shoulders sag in relief at his agreement to keep mum. "Thanks. I owe you."

His intent, frustrated gaze holds hers. "You know he's gonna be pissed as hell at us for keepin' it from him."

She laughs. "At least we'll get bitched out together."

Seth grunts, but his expression softens.

Feeling spent, Sal leans back against the couch. Unbidden, almost unconsciously, her hands drift to her stomach. "I just want it to stick, you know?"

"I know. And it will."

Sal's lips tremble and Seth reaches out, taking her hand in his. He squeezes, his calloused fingers curling around hers as he pulls her in for a hug. Sal closes her eyes, leaning into him, his warmth, and his friendship.

Seth's soft rumbling drawl sweeps over her like a soothing breeze. "Everything's gonna be alright."

chapter
EIGHT

S AL CHANGES OUT OF HER UNIFORM IN THE LOCKER room, smashing the fabric into her duffel bag and pulling out a change of clothes. If she doesn't get out of here now, she's going to be late. She and Luke have plans to watch the Vols game at Jace and Emmy Lou's, and then dinner down on Broadway. Sal dresses quick, slipping on a graphic tee, skinny jeans and black flats. She slips her muted phone in her back pocket, letting out a hiss when she sees the time. Five p.m.

She's late. She's already late and Luke, not to mention Seth, is gonna give her shit all night for her poor punctual performance.

She pauses in front of the mirror to run a hand down her belly. Today, she's twelve weeks. An excited shiver rushes through her. She's planning to tell Luke the news tonight after their dinner. It's been a torturous two weeks of waiting. But now the moment is finally here and she's never been so excited. With Henry, the baby she lost at four months, thanks to her memory loss, she can't remember anything about him. She's seen bump photos, knows she was wracked with morning sickness because Luke told her, but every sensation, every memory is gone. This is a new experience and she's determined to soak up every bit she can. She wants to enjoy it with Luke and stop worrying about jinxing it.

Sal scowls at her reflection in the mirror. *Hear that, dummy? Stop worrying.*

Then she's shouldering her bag, moving for the door. Before she can enter the hall, the door swings open and Tawny enters. "Have fun tonight." She raises a knowing brow. "And good luck."

Sal laughs.

Outside, she crosses the parking lot. The late-afternoon sun is hot, the rush of traffic over the underpass loud. She unlocks her car and slides in, locking the door. She's pulling out her phone to text Luke when there's a tap at her window. She glances up. A stocky man stands at her driver's-side door. He looks nervous, disheveled, his hands in his pockets. "Ma'am, can you help me find someone?"

Sal frowns and slides her phone in her pocket. "I'm sorry," she says loudly to be heard through the glass while sticking her key in the ignition. She gives a calm smile that doesn't betray her nerves at being approached by a stranger. "I can't, but the hospital help desk can."

Every instinct she has is telling her to drive away. *Now. Now, Sal.*

"Sure, of course," the man says, fumbling with something in his pocket. "But one last thing, real quick. Where's Molly Banks?"

Sal's eyes widen. Her heart springs into her throat, her stomach clenching painfully.

She's unprepared for what comes next.

The man moves quick.

He pulls a gun from his pocket. His face twisted, his eyes wild.

All the air rushes from her lungs. Instinctively, Sal raises her hands. "No—please!"

She screams as the window shatters. As everything goes dark.

"Okay, thanks, Tawny. I'll let you know when I hear from her." Luke's gut tightens as he hangs up the phone. Again, for the hundredth time tonight, his eyes drift to the clock on the wall. It's slow, by minutes, but it doesn't matter.

Sal's two hours late. By now, she should be home. When she didn't show up to meet him at the house, he drove by the hospital, saw her car was gone and came back home, figuring he had just missed her or she had gone straight to Jace's. But an hour passed. And then another. No text. No phone call. That isn't like Sal. If she's late, she always lets him know.

Silence fills the house and Luke takes a quick pace around the kitchen. There's a tug in his gut that tells him something ain't right. It ain't right at all.

Still, Luke wrangles his mind back from the edge of the abyss. He ain't going there.

He can't. Not yet.

He chuckles, imagining his wife walking through the front door. Her green eyes wide, her beautiful face apologetic for being late, but ready to tease Luke for sounding the alarms, to scoff at him for being a damn fool.

He picks up his phone again. Scrawls through the texts he's sent to Sal.

Shoot me a text, darlin, let me know you're okay.

Sal, you there?

Sal, you're scarin' me. Where are you?

Luke drifts, phone in his hands. Kitchen. Hallway. Living room.

He sits in the leather recliner beside the couch. Checks his phone for a call from Tawny, who's searching the hospital from top to bottom for Sal. A call from Seth, who failed to answer earlier. His brother's got a date, got a girl, got something not to answer Luke's calls. Hell, with any luck Sal's with him. Hopefully.

He gets up and paces to the mantel. He closes his eyes, trying to gather himself. But he can't stop his plummeting heart. The house is quiet. Too quiet. The feeling is eerily similar to when he returned to Nashville without Sal. After Florida. After the plane crash where she went missing. How many times has he thought about that night? Coming home to an empty house after the failed search and rescue, Seth and Jace camped out in guest bedrooms. Expecting her to come around a corner at any moment, but all there was was a whisper of her smell, the ghosts of her absence. And how many times has he thanked his goddamn lucky stars above, thanked god, thanked anyone that would listen when Sal came home. When she returned to him.

And now . . .

Gone.

She's gone.

This can't be happening again.

But it is. Luke can feel it.

He braces his hands against the fireplace mantel, his brain short-circuiting at the thought. This isn't normal. Nothing about this is normal. Something happened to her.

Someone did something to her.

Glancing down, Luke traces a thumb across the tattoo on his palm, on that snap of connection he shares with Sal. Almost as if it can help him find her.

There's a heaviness in his chest, a tug pulling him toward her. He just doesn't know where she is. All he knows is he's got to do something.

His phone goes off.

Fumbling, frantic, Luke pulls his cell from his back pocket. It's not her name, but it's the next best person. He exhales and slides the screen to answer.

"Seth."

"Hey, man, I know I missed the game, but—"

Luke cuts him off. "I can't find Sal." He closes his eyes. Words he never thought he'd hear again. Words that threaten to take him to the fucking grave.

There's a long pause. Luke wants his brother to tell him to cool his jets. To tell him that he's overreacting.

Instead, there's a hitch of Seth's breath. His voice, tight and constricted, hits Luke's ears like a balm. "I'm on my way."

S AL SWEARS AS SHE'S PULLED FROM THE TRUNK of her car. She stumbles, is caught by rough hands. She blinks her eyes in surprise. It's as dark outside as it was in the trunk.

Her brain tries to remember. She had woken up, what, fifteen, thirty minutes after being knocked out with the butt of the gun? Her foggy mind searches the myriad of sounds she heard when she was in the trunk. The rumble of train tracks. Two sets. No rush of freeway traffic, so back roads. Backwoods? Farm?

"Move, bitch." The man shoves her in the direction of a small cabin. Sal walks on legs of jelly as she's practically dragged over the gravel drive.

A groan leaves her lips. Her head hurts, pounding out a fierce beat of a headache. She can feel the dried blood on her temple, streaming down the side of her head. Her hands are tied in front of her. Tight, but not too tight.

She uses the walk to clock her surroundings. It's too dark to see much, but she can hear birds in their roosts. The howl of freight trains in the distance. Water, far off, somewhere. The outlines of tall trees reaching the sky. Forest?

Sal stumbles as her world tilts and blurs, but there's only a grunt and she's marched forward.

She dares a glance at the guy who had busted the glass on the car window. He's short, stocky, with a mean expression, greasy shoulder-length hair and a goatee.

It's Molly Banks's husband. She knows it without a doubt. He's brought her here to make her talk. To find Molly. To kill her? She closes her eyes at the thought. Nausea churns her gut, but she forces herself to stay strong. Stay alert.

Vibration after vibration comes from her back pocket. She coughs to cover the sound. Luke. She knows it's him. God, what this will do to him. He'll be so worried. But, hope surges in her, he'll know. He'll know something's wrong. He'll come for her.

The man shoves her through a heavy wooden door. Immediately, they're in the kitchen. Two toppled chairs, dishes stacked in the sink, beer cans on the counter. She shivers. It reminds her of the house she shared with Roy. Small, claustrophobic, creepy. Blue curtains hang on the window. Pictures on the fridge. Fluorescent lighting. Creaky floorboards. It's a home. Most likely Molly's and her husband's.

She concentrates hard, getting it all down in her memory so she can put this fucker in a jail cell.

Her attention's jerked back to the present, when she's shoved into a kitchen chair. "Sit," the man commands, thrusting a gun in her face. "Stay."

"Chris? It's Chris, right?" Sal says, searching her

memory. In the light of the kitchen, Sal notes he's wearing a crisp white polo tucked into khaki Carhartts. The gun's shoved in his waistband.

He slicks black hair behind his ears. "Yeah."

"Why am I here?" It's a feat of strength to keep calm, keep cool. But she forces herself to. Be polite. Play dumb. Just long enough to get out of here alive.

"You know why you're here." He shifts his weight. "You made my wife leave. You made Molly leave me."

Sal tilts her head. Turns on some of the training she learned. Active listening. Summon empathy. Even though she aches to hit him. To swing her fist like she did at Roy in their final confrontation. She knows it's best to play small now, so she can play smart later. "You sound pretty hurt about that."

"Sure, I'm fucking hurt!" Chris's nostrils flare. His eyes swivel to a dark corner in the kitchen, where, Sal's stunned to see, crouches a midsized scruffy terrier dog. "All I got now is this damn mutt."

With an almost comical pirouette, Chris spins around and kicks at the dog. Sal winces at the pained yelp that comes from the animal, digging her nails in her palms to keep her anger at bay. The dog skitters across the floor, baring its teeth in a growl, its long nails clacking as it disappears into another room.

"Stupid dog," Chris mutters, his focus drifting back to Sal, his face smoothing out into a mask. Contrite. Calm. He opens his hands. "Let's start over. I just want to make sure Molly's okay. Please. All I care about is my wife." From his back pocket he pulls out his cell phone, an ancient flip phone, and shows it to Sal. "This is all I got left of her. My only way to reach her."

Control her, Sal thinks.

But she keeps quiet. A strange kind of anger welling in her. She knows men like this. Knows what they'll do. Lie. Gaslight. Act like they care right before they treat you like a dog. Well, she's not a dog. Not anymore.

Sal's eyes land on the back door. An exit. Locked.

Chris holds his waistband and tries for a smile. "It's super simple. Tell me where she is and I'll let you go."

Sal's stomach clenches. It'd be so easy to tell him where Molly is, but she can't. A year ago, she was Molly. And ever since then, she made herself a promise to keep that strength she found. To live a life that was true and honest. She'll never go back there. Never make another woman experience what she did. If Chris gets Molly back, he'd kill her. Sal knows it. She couldn't live with herself if that happened.

"I don't know," she says with a shake of her head. "I don't know where she is."

"Liar!" he yells into her face. "You fucking bitch. You know. I know you helped her. She told me all about you. The nice nurse from the hospital. So fucking helpful."

"Paramedic, asshole," Sal shoots back, unable to help herself.

It's a mistake.

Sal sees the fury on his face and her eyes go wide. He's wheeled back, his fist ready to strike, to hit, to hammer everywhere, her stomach included. Sal hunches over, her bound hands flying to her stomach.

The words are out of her mouth before she can stop them. A blurt of fear, a plea: "Please don't. I'm pregnant."

Chris freezes, an eerie smile spreading across his face. Sal's heart sinks at what she's just done.

She's given him ammunition.

"Fine. Don't talk." He stands over her, breathing unevenly, his fists releasing. He leans close and grips her chin. "This is your own damn fault."

With that, Chris grabs her roughly by the arm and wrenches her from her seat. He yanks her forward and shoves her toward an open door.

Shit, Sal thinks when she sees where they're headed. The basement. They descend the stairs. It takes all Sal has not to fight, to struggle, but she can't risk Chris's wrath. A shove down the stairs. An accidental fall. God, she can't chance that. She closes her eyes. She can't risk her baby.

Chris's dull monotone takes her from her thoughts. "On the ground."

Sal obeys, sitting with her back against the wall as he ties her binds to the radiator pipe. It's an uncomfortable position, with her arms pulled up and to the side, but she bites her tongue, refusing to give the bastard the satisfaction of knowing she's in pain.

Chris stands, breathing unevenly as he stares down at her. "You'll talk. Or you'll stay here until you do."

With that, he turns. The echo of his footsteps is loud up the stairs. Sal flinches at the sound of the slamming door, the basement cast in unbearable darkness. *Fuck you,* she thinks. She jerks frantically against the binds, her eyes taking in the barren basement, the cinderblock walls, the scattered tools on the floor, the door on the opposite side of the wall. The only source of light comes from a high window. And outside, all she can see is the moon, remote—far away from everyone she knows and loves.

Pure panic. The house is pure panic and Luke's drowning.

He paces his worry all over the house. By now, he's called the cops. They had him make a report, and advised him to call friends and family, and then told him to sit tight while they work on getting around to it. The message was clear—maybe she forgot to charge her phone, maybe she got a flat, maybe give it a little more time. It wasn't their top priority.

But it sure as hell is Luke's.

After he hung up with the cops, he drove all over the city looking for Sal. Finally, he came home, empty-handed. Hoping against hope that Sal was there.

She wasn't.

But Seth and Jace were. His brother and best friend had been in the driveway when he pulled up to the house, their expressions grim but determined.

Now, Jace is on the phone with Sal's sister. He can hear Lacey's voice getting more panicked, more insistent with each detail Jace gives out.

Which isn't much.

Seth prowls by the living room window. "So what do we do now? Just sit here and wait?" His voice comes out utterly frustrated. Luke knows it's killing Seth just as much as it's killing him—the waiting, the god-awful helplessness.

"Tawny said she was on her way home," Luke says, ripping a frustrated hand through his hair. He feels ready to jump out of his skin. "Sal was changed and ready for the game. That's all I know. That's all I goddamn got."

He's aware Seth's watching him carefully. Looking for signs he's falling apart. Which he isn't. He can't. Not when Sal's out there.

Luke stares out the window. It's dark, nearing ten o'clock, the moon bright and high in the sky. The thought of Sal out there, alone, is too much for him to take.

"Luke?" A chirp of a voice sounds. He turns. Emmy Lou's sticking her blonde head out of the kitchen. She's been cooking away her worry the entire night. "Do you want coffee with your cake?" she asks, her pretty face pained.

Jace sighs, tucking his cell in his back pocket. "Stop cookin', Em. No one's eatin.'"

"I have to do something, Jace," she whispers like Luke can't hear. "What else do we do?"

Her words have Luke's heartbeat ratcheting up in his chest. So damn fast at first he thinks he's having a heart attack on the spot, but then he realizes it's the sound of his heartbeat ticking down because the woman he loves is missing.

Luke closes his eyes. Emmy Lou's right. Everything's taking too long.

Seth edges close, gesturing for him to step into the hallway, out of earshot. "Luke, I gotta tell you somethin.'"

Luke stares at his brother. "What is it?" Seth's pale. His eyes dull with pain.

Seth's throat bobs. "It's about Sal. She's—"

The front door cracks.

Jace's head whips up as Emmy Lou makes a squeak of alarm.

Luke's heart lurches in his chest, and he's striding forward, fast, but—

It's Griff Greyson. He's stepping through the front door, closely followed by Alabama. Both of them wear expressions of sympathy. "Luke," Alabama says, squeezing his arm. "Have you heard from her yet?"

All he can manage is a shake of his head. Anything else will have him dissolving. Choking up.

"C'mon," Jace says, steering him away from Alabama's sad eyes.

They all gather in the kitchen. Griff evaluates the freshly baked pies, the phone numbers scrawled on notepads, the stacked *Nashville Stars*. He crosses his tattooed arms. "Sal wasn't goin' anywhere?"

Luke grips the back of his neck. "No. We had plans to watch the game. She was on her way home, goddamnit . . ."

He breaks off, sick of explaining, of trying to find answers, when even he doesn't know what the hell's going on. He's been wracking his brain the last few hours, trying to play connect the dots over the last couple of days. If Sal had mentioned anything, if she had said something he failed to remember. But nothing. All he gets for it is unbearable guilt, the knowledge that something happened to Sal and he's the one who failed to keep her safe. The one thing he always promised her.

There's a hand on Luke's shoulder, Jace's calm hazel eyes on his reminding him to take a breath. "We'll find her," Jace says.

Griff tucks Alabama against him. "What about the cops?"

"Useless," Seth mutters.

Luke needles his brow. "What they're doin' to find her it's . . . it's not enough. And I ain't trustin' them with Sal, not when they fucked up everything the last time." He inhales. "It's been almost four hours. She'd be home by now. And she ain't, because something happened."

Griff stares at him, his face tight. "Tell us what to do, Kincaid." Beside him, Alabama nods, her face set and determined.

The offer nearly chokes him up. The people that he needs are here for him and Sal. Asking him what they can do to help, and telling him they'll do it.

Christ, he's never been so goddamn grateful.

Luke shakes off indecision and glances at the friends around him. Everyone's waiting. High-energy, tense. Ready to work. "We look. Again," he says fiercely. "We drive around. We go back to the hospital. We look some more. I ain't sleepin' till she's home."

"Fuck yes," Griff growls.

Emmy Lou, cleaning off the counter, swipes her thin arm, sweeping napkins and tabloids into the trash. As Luke's eyes light on the newspaper, an idea hits him like a lightning bolt.

He grins and looks at Seth. "We tell the *Star*."

"Shit," Seth says, his eyes wide.

Jace nods, sucking in a breath. "Hell, that's a goddamn good idea."

Luke exhales, coming alive. A surge of adrenaline at finally having a damn plan. "Get it all over the news. Sal's missing."

"Y'all think it'll work?" Alabama asks.

"It has to," Luke says, already pulling out his phone.

For once in his life, he can't wait for Sal to be front-page news. The *Star* will put his wife out there. For someone to find. For Luke to bring home.

TEN

S AL MAY BE DOWN, DOWN IN A BASEMENT TO BE exact, but she's not out. Hell no.

She's pissed as hell and ready to get out of this place.

She sets to work. Makes a game plan. First, get out of these binds. Second, get her phone. Third, get home and kiss her husband like crazy.

Tears prick the back of her eyelids. She has to get out of here. For herself. For her baby. She closes her eyes. For Luke. He's over the edge. She can feel it.

Sal struggles against her binds. They're thick rope and tied haphazardly. Chris may be an abusive asshole, but he's hardly smart. He thinks with his fists, not his brain.

She listens to the old cabin. It's silent. Her eyes survey her exit options. A high, narrow basement window. There's no way to boost herself up, and she doubts she could fit. The only other option left is the way she came in. Up the stairs, through the kitchen, and out the door. And then where?

It doesn't matter. Anywhere is better than here.

At the crack of a door, Sal bristles. She braces herself for Chris, but all she gets is heavy breathing. The soft trot of paws down the stairs.

Sal lets out a little laugh.

It's the dog.

He's shuffling through the darkened basement, through milky moonlight, making for Sal. She swears under her breath, unsure if he's friendly or not.

After a beat or two, the scruffy thing approaches her, his tongue lolling out of his mouth in a goofy expression. He's scrawny and needs a good brushing, but his eyes are soft and dark and inquisitive. When he bumps his wet nose against Sal's hand, nuzzling it with a muffled snuffle, she realizes the growl he let loose earlier was meant for Chris. And Chris alone.

Sal makes a clicking with her tongue. "Hey, boy. How you doing?"

He sits down beside her, his tail wagging across the cold cement. She squints in the dim light, trying to make out a name on the collar. Winston.

Well, now, she's got a dog for company. At least she's not talking to herself anymore.

"What do you think, Winston?" Sal asks, getting up on her knees. "We gonna get out of here?" She gives her body a careful wrench, not wanting to jar the cell phone in her back pocket. She'll need it later.

The rope loosens. Barely. She grits her teeth, twists again.

A low woof rumbles out of Winston.

Amused, she gives him the side-eye. "Oh sure, I'm taking you with me. Don't worry. I wouldn't leave you behind." When the rope refuses to budge, she sinks back down the wall and lets out a heavy sigh. "Don't suppose you can dial me up 911 or fetch me a pocketknife?"

His dark, solemn eyes stare back at her as if to say *I am but a mere dog, silly woman.*

The creaking of the floorboard has Winston standing on all fours, a low growl rising up in his throat. Sal scoots back against the wall.

There's movement on the stairs, and then Chris appears in the basement. Silent, drifting, like a ghost. Sal sees he's traded the gun for a knife. The memory of Roy rears its head, but she forces it away.

Chris stops in front of her. "Are you ready to talk, bitch?"

"Maybe," she lies. "Can I use the bathroom first?"

He considers her request. A strange smile overtakes his face. He kneels in front of her, his meaty hands going to her binds. "You try something, I'll stab you in the stomach."

Sal shivers, his threat too cruel to contemplate.

She stares at him, hating him, her thoughts murderous, wishing she could drive the knife through his face. She's not that forgiving. You take her from her husband, her friends, put her child in danger, hell yes, she'll think violent thoughts.

She licks dry lips. "I promise."

She's untied from the pipe and yanked to her feet. When Chris grips her arm and pulls her forward, Sal's heart drops. Instead of being taken upstairs, she's led to the door on the opposite wall. Any hopes of using her phone are dashed. She's in a basement. It'll be a miracle if she has service.

Sal pauses in the doorway, thrusting her hands toward Chris. "I need these off," she says, lifting her chin, using all of her bravado. "I'll pee all over myself."

Scowling, Chris loosens the binds and shoves her inside the bathroom. "Five minutes," he warns, leveling a finger at her. "Then I'm coming in."

The door shuts.

Sal depresses the lock. Turns on the faucet. Breathes.

Then she pulls out her phone.

Two bars. It's enough. It has to be.

With frantic, numb fingers she punches her speed dial. She knows she should be calling 911, but fuck it. She needs her husband's voice to get her through this. She needs Luke. She has to tell him in case it's too late.

Luke.

It's all over the news.

Sal's missing.

Right now, Luke couldn't love the press more. Sal's in trouble and people are looking.

It's been hours. Emmy Lou, Jace and Alabama stayed at the house, communicating with the *Star*, while Luke, Seth and Griff went back to the hospital. Meeting with a dead end there, they scoured the streets of Nashville once more, looking for her car, questioning anyone they could.

Now it's late, and everyone's gathered in the living

room. Above the fireplace mantel, the TV flickers its fluorescent glow. Luke's kept it on mute. He can't handle the perky voices, relaying something so grim yet loving the juicy scoop they've just been handed. It's torture enough seeing Sal's photo splashed across the screen. Her beautiful face selling sorrow. It's something he never wanted to relive in a million years.

Still, he's hoping it works. That someone sees and calls something in. Anything.

"You can't do that somewhere else?" Seth gripes from his place at the window.

Emmy Lou, curled up on the couch, looks up from filing her nails. "What?"

"It's not a goddamn day spa," Seth snaps. "Sal's missin.'"

Jace frowns, glances over at his wife, whose pretty face is bewildered and hurt. "Seth, easy," he says in a low voice.

"I have to do somethin'," Emmy Lou whispers to Jace, tears in her eyes. "I'm sorry, I didn't know . . ."

Seth grumbles again.

"All of y'all calm the hell down," Griff growls, taking up for Luke. He sits in one of the leather recliners, Alabama perched on his lap.

From his place by the fireplace, Luke sighs, sweeping his tired gaze across the living room. With no new leads found, everyone's exhausted, on edge. Seth especially. His brother's been quiet all night, focused, worrying. Needing to stay busy, to do something, but they've already scoured half of Nashville, pretty much put out their own APB with the *Star*. What else is there to do? Sit around and fucking wait?

Luke looks over to say something, to rein Seth in, only the ringing of his phone has Luke glancing down.

His heart almost stops when he sees who it is.

"It's Sal," he says hoarsely.

There's a stunned silence, the sound of Emmy Lou's gasp, and then all the boots in the house are standing and barreling across the wood floor. Seth has his hands behind the back of his head, Jace's signaling for Luke to put it on speakerphone.

He does, and answers.

"Sal?" His voice breaks when he says her name.

"Luke?" Her smoky voice is a wisp of a whisper over the line. An angel, his saving grace when he needs it the most.

He braces himself against the mantel, his pulse rocketing, everything going laser-focused, every person in the room falling away. Every question at the forefront of his mind leaping into his mouth. "Jesus, Sal. Where are you? What happened? Are you okay?"

"I don't know . . . I don't know where I am . . . took me . . ."

God no. His heart plummets on her last word. It's worse than he thought. Her car didn't break down, her phone didn't die. Someone took her.

Out of the corner of his eye, Seth stands still, head bowed, jaw clenched.

Rage, furious and venomous, licks over Luke. He grips his phone so tight he could snap it in half. "Who took you?"

"—olly's . . . band . . . Chris . . . from the hospital."

Luke strains to listen. Her voice is tinny over the line, their connection tenuous. "Are you okay? Are you hurt?"

Briefly, he catches the eye of Griff, who's already on his phone with the cops.

"I'm okay . . . I'm not hurt, but . . . I don't have long . . . in the bathroom . . ."

Luke takes a deep breath, fighting fear, frustration. The information she's giving isn't helping him any thanks to the goddamn reception. "Sal, darlin', I ain't hearin' you so well." He keeps his voice light, calm, even though he feels desperate as hell. "Can you try again and tell me where you are?"

"Hold on." There's the rustle of movement, a shower curtain crunching, and then her voice is back, clearer. ". . . passed over train tracks . . . two of them. We're in the woods somewhere. A cabin. And there's a—"

She breaks off.

He swears. All he wants is a location. Anything to find her and the universe ain't even giving him that much. "Okay, that's good, darlin', what else?"

"I don't know, I can't—"

"It's okay." Luke squeezes his eyes shut, his fist. "We're comin' for you, d'you hear me, Sal? Listen to me. We're gonna find you."

"I know. I know. Oh, I'm sorry," she says, tearfully. "I'm so sorry, Luke. I should've told you . . . I—"

"Sal?"

A suck of her breath. And then—

Sal screams. "Oh no! No!"

A split second later, the sound of wood breaking. A dog's frantic barks. And then the line goes dead.

"Sal!" Luke roars into the phone.

Gripping it in a stranglehold, his last lifeline to Sal gone, Luke stares at his phone in horror until Jace pries it away. Numbly, he watches as Jace, his hands shaky, his face pale, dials back Sal's number. His best friend listens, swallows, says, "Phone's been turned off."

Luke wrenches his eyes shut and turns away. He smears his face in his hands. Trying to breathe. Trying to live. His heart in a million pieces. He is broken. A broken fucking man.

"Got the cops on the line, Kincaid," Griff says, stretching out his cell phone, his face drawn in deep anger.

A pained sound comes from Seth. "Luke."

"It's gotta wait," Luke bites out, holding up a hand to silence his brother. He grabs Griff's phone, only to find he's been placed on hold. A frustrated growl rolls out of Luke.

"It can't wait. It's really fuckin' important."

He lifts his gaze to Seth. Luke's stomach clenches at what he sees in his brother's face. Worry. Agony. Seth's pale and shaking. "Goddamnit, what is it?" He grips his brother's shoulder. "You're scarin' me."

"It's Sal. What she was trying to tell you." Seth swallows, meets his eyes. "She's pregnant."

Alabama says softly, "Oh, no."

"Holy shit," Jace breathes.

Luke freezes, staring at Seth in confusion. "What?"

"She's pregnant, man." Seth hangs his head, his voice splintering. "She found out two weeks ago."

Luke's mind works to put it all together, to register the bomb of information of Seth's just dropped, but he can't. The world tilts out from under him. "No," he chokes out. He leans forward, grabbing his knees. Griff shoves a chair toward him and Jace hauls him back. Luke barely makes it into a sitting position where he folds over, burying his face in his hands. Tears burn his eyelids.

Pregnant. Sal's pregnant.

When he looks up, he finds Seth kneeling in front of him, waiting in the silence of the stricken living room.

Seth's haunted-eyed gaze finds his, and when Luke exhales, says, "Tell me," Seth wipes his face, nods his head and says, "Okay."

chapter
ELEVEN

L UKE WRAPS HIS HANDS AROUND THE BACK PORCH railing, stares dazedly out into the early morning. Dawn on the horizon. The river glitters with the arrival of the sun. Nearly twelve hours since Sal's gone missing. A torture Luke can barely withstand.

By now, because of Sal's phone call, the cops are taking it seriously. They've come to the house, taken statements and left. Left Luke with reassurances that they're doing all they can to find his wife. Left Luke with instructions to wait while they work.

But he can't. All he can do is think about that phone call, the phone call that threatened to bring him to his knees. Sal's scream, the door breaking, shattering, is like a thread of terror ringing in his ears. The mere thought of Sal going through something like this again, when she's survived so much, has him sick to his stomach.

And the kicker of it all—

She's pregnant.

It should be his greatest joy; instead, it's his worst nightmare. He's fucking terrified. The thought of her alone, hurt, kept somewhere, worrying about the baby, about him.

He can't even imagine what Sal's going through. They've wanted it for so long, but all Luke can focus on is his wife. Once he gets her back, he'll do everything under the sun to tell her how goddamn happy he is, but right now her safety—their safety—is the only thing that matters.

Footsteps behind him and Luke turns.

Not surprisingly, it's Seth. His brother's been giving him space since he dropped the bombshell, but he's been there, in the margins, waiting, and now wears an agonized expression.

"If you wanna take a swing at me, you can." Seth holds his hands out as he steps toward Luke. "I kinda want to kick my own ass to tell you the truth."

Luke sighs. "I ain't gonna hit you. I sure as hell wish you woulda told me. Hell, I wish she woulda told me."

Seth lowers his head and nods. "I know. I sure am sorry, Luke."

The guilt and pain in his voice has Luke feeling for Seth. Because his brother was going through hell tonight. Knowing Sal was gone, knowing she was pregnant and trying to keep her secret until he couldn't any longer. That's Seth. Loyal as hell. A pain in his ass.

Luke drags in a rough breath. "Right now, I don't care about any of that. I just want her home. I want her to be okay. I want—"

He breaks off, his throat knotting with grief. He can't force the words out. Can't bear to entertain any other thoughts other than Sal home with him. Safe.

Seth places a hand on Luke's shoulder. Squeezes.

At the sound of a doorbell, the tinny chime floating

faintly onto the back porch, Luke stiffens. Groans. "It's the cops."

But when he and Seth retreat inside, he's surprised to see a young girl in the foyer. Tears in her eyes, a knapsack dropped on the floor, wringing her hands as she speaks in low tones to Alabama and Griff.

Luke frowns. "What is this?"

"Luke," Jace says, hustling over, his face flushed. "You want to talk to her."

Griff turns, snaps his fingers. "Now, Kincaid."

"Sit down, honey." Alabama guides the girl out of the hallway to a kitchen chair. There, everyone assembles, looking to Luke as he enters, Seth on his heels. Alabama lasers her gray eyes to Luke. "Luke, this is Molly Banks."

The girl's eyes widen at the appearance of Luke. "It's my fault. She tried to help me."

Luke swallows and steps forward. "Who tried to help you?"

"Sal. Your wife. I saw it on the news—she's missing?" When Luke nods, she whimpers. "I didn't listen. I went back to the house after she told me not to. Chris knew. He knew I was trying to leave. I got out, but—I know he went after her."

"Oh, fuck," Seth says somewhere across the room.

Instantly, Luke lights on the brief conversation he and Sal had days ago. The girl she helped. The girl who reminded her of Roy. Fuck. That was it. He had it all along, in the recesses of his mind—he had it and he just didn't know it.

"It's all my fault," Molly moans. "I told him about her."

"Who'd you tell?" Luke asks in a low voice.

"My husband. Chris. He was so angry. He said he'd find

her if he couldn't find me." Molly bursts into sobs. "He's going to hurt her. I know it."

"Christ," Griff mutters.

Seth and Jace exchange frantic glances.

Despite Molly's words, hope jumps in Luke's chest. He's close. Close to finding Sal. Slowly, he sits across from the girl. "Molly, where is she? Where'd he take her?"

"To our house."

"Where the hell is that?" Seth snaps, impatient.

"Seth," Jace hisses, his expression grim.

The girl shrinks back and Luke fights to control his temper, his worry. "Listen," he says quietly, not wanting to spook her. He focuses solely on Molly. On this girl who holds the key to where his wife is. "It's really important we find her before something bad happens to her. Please."

Everyone's holding their breath.

Finally, she nods. "We live in Ashland City—1125 Hillside Drive." She sticks her hands between her legs, shivers. "A cabin with little blue shutters. There's a well out back. A dirt road."

"That's only thirty minutes away," Jace says, already calling up a map on his phone.

Luke rockets to standing, and for a moment, it feels as if the past has its hands in the future.

Then he strides to the closet and rips out the shotgun.

Griff's eyes go wide. "Whoa, what are you doin', Kincaid?"

"Goddamnit, Luke." Jace groans as if he already knows how it's gonna go down. "The cops said if anything happens—"

"Fuck the cops," Luke snaps. "My wife's out there and I ain't waitin.'"

He damn sure is breaking all the rules in the law book. The longer they wait, the longer Sal's in danger. He ain't taking any chances. He's got to find her. Find her okay. Find her fast.

Luke looks to Alabama, knowing she can handle what he won't do. "You call the cops and tell 'em where we are. I ain't sittin' around to wait on this. I'm goin' to get Sal."

Griff steps forward, his face ready for a fight. "You ain't goin' alone."

Alabama loops her arm through Griff's, keeping him still, keeping him with her, but glances at Luke. "Y'all ain't doing this." Her Texas drawl's a tremble. Fear etched all over her pale face.

Griff turns to her, placating. "Sweetheart . . ."

There's a glint in Griff's tawny eyes, and in that instant Luke knows they're not just friends anymore. They're family. Griff's willing to put his life on the line for Sal and that's saying everything.

But Luke also can't let him do that.

"You ain't," Luke says, putting out a hand to stop Griff. "I am."

Relief clouds Alabama's face and she throws Luke a grateful look.

Luke glances at Seth, who's already moving for the door, and says in a firm tone, "Seth, sit down and stay here."

Seth's mouth flatlines. "The hell I am."

"Stay," Luke commands, his expression fierce.

Griff gives a nod. "Go get her, Kincaid."

With that, Luke slams out the screen door, shoots out

of the house faster than a cannonball. He's halfway to his truck when the screen door rattles again. He whips around. "Go back inside, Seth."

His brother gets hurt, he'll never forgive himself.

"Man, fuck you," comes Seth's resolved rumble. His boots pound down the steps to stand tall in front of Luke. No regret in his eyes. Only resolve. "It's Sal, and I ain't sittin' this out."

They lock eyes, Seth's burning bright, and Luke's at a loss for words. He knows he's got no chance in hell of talking Seth out of this. Sal and Luke and Seth always had each other's back and Seth ain't backing down now. Not when Sal needs him. Not when she's in trouble. And not when Luke needs him.

"C'mon," Luke says. "We gotta find her fast."

They stride forward.

The screen door clatters.

Luke groans. "Not you too."

Jace is smirking. "Ain't gonna get far without these." He holds up the keys to the truck.

Luke swears and then nods at Jace. He sees what his best friend's telling him. They do this together. Like their band. Their brotherhood. "Fine. But I'm drivin.'"

They're in the truck fast and gone.

Luke's heart flickers like an ember, and he can almost feel Sal, calling his name, as he steers the truck down the dusty dirt road.

I'm comin' for you, Sal. Do you hear me, darlin'? We're comin'.

chapter
TWELVE

I T'S FIVE A.M. THAT'S SAL'S FIRST THOUGHT AS SHE comes to on the dirty basement floor. She knows the turn of the sun, its golden slant, from all her early-morning runs.

Her head hurts. That's her second thought. She feels as if her entire skull's been cleaved in with an axe. She groans as her memory of the night before returns. Chris catching her with the cell phone. He was enraged, realizing what she had been doing, and yanked her out of the shower by her hair, slammed her up against the wall before she even had time to fight back.

Then, blackout.

She must have slept it off all night. Unconsciousness giving way to an uneasy sleep.

Still, the risk was worth it. Just to hear Luke's voice. Electric, soothing and frantic all at once. She doesn't know if she gave him enough information to find her, but she clings to his voice. The conversation gave her hope she needed that she'll get out of this.

Sal presses herself up on her hands and the world whirls in front of her. Her ears ring. She tastes blood in her mouth, knows her lip's cut and swollen, but tells herself it can be stitched up later. Everything can come later. Telling Luke about the baby, getting medical attention, right now she has to get out.

There's movement in the corner of the basement and then Chris is stepping out of the shadows. Nausea churns in her stomach. She doesn't know how long he's been there, watching, waiting.

He hasn't bothered to tie her up. And that tells her all she needs to know. He plans to kill her. Well, joke's on him because she's pissed as hell and ready to get out of this place. She doesn't plan on dying today. She's got a baby on the way. A husband at home who's waiting on her.

"That was a stupid, stupid idea," Chris says. "And you're a stupid, stupid woman."

He prowls above her. Agitated, aggressive. The mask's finally fallen. He's no longer friendly. No more the loving, adoring husband. Sal's probably seeing what Molly saw. Every damn day.

Chris clutches his phone to him like it's a lifeline to Molly. Which, to him, in his demented mind, it probably is. His phone's the only way to find her now. Control her.

Chris stops his pacing. Swift, he squats in front of Sal and thrusts the knife in her direction. "I want you to call her. Call Molly. Now."

Sal trembles as she presses herself back against the cinderblock wall. A crazed laugh bubbles in her throat and she can't help but let it loose. She's trapped with a man with a knife to her throat. She always believed in second chances, but not this again.

Never again.

"You laughing at me?" Chris seethes. "You think it's funny? You think it's fucking funny?"

With the swiftness of a snake, Chris levels the tip of the knife inches from her stomach. In a voice as deadly as a dagger, he asks, "You think *this* is funny?"

"No," Sal says, her hands flying to her stomach as if they're steel. As if she can protect the baby within from the cold tip of the blade. She feels faint, a hollow ringing like an alarm in her ears.

He holds out his phone. "Call her. And no fake numbers either. I'm fucking onto you. You sneaky bitch. You sneaky little bitch."

As she stares at the man in front of her, rage electrifies her like a snapping wire. He's crazy. He's coming undone without Molly. Without a way to get to her. The need to have her, the need to beat the shit out of Sal converging.

Sal has to play this smart if she wants to get out of here alive. The way he's acting, it won't take much to set him off. But maybe that's what she wants to do. Piss him off. Catch him off guard. Run.

Sal's eyes move to the stairs. To the basement door that's been left open.

She has to take the chance. If she waits any longer, she won't make it. Her and her baby, they both won't make it. She didn't kill Roy only to go down like this.

One last chance.

"Fine," Sal says. With trembling hands, she takes his phone, Luke's face in her mind. Her baby's heartbeat in her ears.

And then she snaps the flip phone in half.

"No!" Chris bellows, his eyes bugging with horror.

"Eat shit, asshole," Sal rasps out and then jams the antenna into his right eye. As hard as she can. It connects with a slurp, and Chris lets out a bloodcurdling scream. His hands fly to his face as he launches himself at her, kicking and screaming. Aiming for her stomach.

Sal's ready. She rolls onto her side, curling up into a tight ball to shield her belly. She yelps in pain as his foot connects with her rib.

Blindly, she fumbles, reaching for anything within her grasp. Her hand curls around a screwdriver. She rolls onto her back, rolls into the kick, and slams the screwdriver's sharp tip into Chris's shin.

His scream pierces the air.

Chris topples to the ground while Sal scrambles up.

The world spins. Her head's on fire. Which way is out? *Oh god, go, Sal. Move your ass. Get out. Go. Go.*

Go where? Anywhere.

And then she's racing up the stairs, a rush of adrenaline and panic as she staggers through the kitchen, her eyes lasered on the back door. She fumbles with the lock, fumbles like a fool from those awful horror movies her sister loves, and then—the lock pops.

Exhilarated, Sal whips open the back door only to find a screen door.

"Noooo," she moans, almost screaming in frustration when she finds that locked as well.

Then she hears Chris pounding up the stairs behind her. Lumbering, screaming in pure rage. He flies into the kitchen, slashing the knife.

Sal goes rigid and braces herself for the blow, but there's a black blur, and then there's Winston, leaping between her and Chris. The mangy mutt is now a beast and he lets loose a vicious snarl before savagely burying his teeth in Chris's thigh.

Chris cries out, staggering backward as he tries to shake Winston loose.

It's all the time Sal needs.

She gets the lock open, the screen door open, and then she's free.

"Get the fuckin' lead out, Luke." Seth sits on the edge of his seat, long fingers drumming the dash, his leg bouncing anxiously.

Luke grits his teeth, bites back his retort. He's pushing the truck as fast as it can go. His nerves are lit and on fire. His attention laser-focused. Focused on finding Sal. Worrying about what's been done to her. Trying not to let fear and panic take over. Because Luke knows Sal will fight. She'll never stop.

Jace swears at the map blinking bright on his phone. "Goddamn reception." He shakes his phone as if giving it a reboot. Extends a finger. "Should be off Route Five here."

"There!" Seth slams a fist against the dash when the sign for Ashland City appears. He sits back, his face stunned. "Sal was right. Two train tracks."

Luke jerks the wheel to the right. The truck bounces as it flies over a pothole and then his pulse kicks up when he sees the cabin in the distance. Gravel road. Blue shutters.

"Middle of fuckin' nowhere," Seth mutters.

Luke grips the wheel and punches the gas. He can feel the adrenaline pounding in his veins.

The truck speeds ahead. Close. So damn close.

Almost there, Sal.

"What do we do when we get there, Luke?" Jace's quiet voice interjects.

Luke clears his mind. After a second glance at Seth, whose jaw is tight in solidarity, he says, "Whatever we have to."

Sal bolts out the back door and into the brightening sky. Sunrise. Pinks and golds and purples. Colors that are certainly cheerier than her current situation.

It's hard keeping her balance, and her sense of direction is off, but she's free. She takes off into the woods, concentrating on finding a road, civilization. Concentrating on not letting her body take over. She knows it wants to shut down. Knows shock is on the horizon. Because she's stressed and she's tired. She tired as hell.

Push. Move, Sal. You can rest when it's over. In fact, there will be nothing but rest because Luke will never let you out of the house again.

At the thought of her husband, Sal balls a fist and readies her feet to fly.

She run-limps over loam. Dark branches like gnarled witch fingers graze the golden sky; her breath comes in herky-jerky gasps. She keeps a hand over her belly as she runs, a reminder, her motivation never to stop, to give it her all.

Bolting left, Sal stumbles, trips over thick scrub, rights

herself. But when she exits the thick grove of trees, what she sees makes her want to break down and bawl like a baby.

Her eyes wide, she turns around and around, staring at the sky, her surroundings.

Holy shit. The cabin.

She's back at the cabin.

She made a full damn circle.

"Oh, Jesus," Sal moans, dipping low to catch her breath. Her knees want to give out. Her lungs are on fire, black spots doing a dance in her vision.

That's when she hears it. An engine. A truck.

Sal's head snaps up.

Luke.

Luke's knuckles go white on the wheel.

Emerging from the cover of trees is Sal. He can't stop the fear, the relief, he feels as he takes in his wife. Limping, her long dark hair disheveled, looking tired and tiny as she braces her palms on her knees and hangs her head.

"There, there, there!" Seth slams his palm on the dash as if Luke doesn't see her. As if his own damn heart isn't fracturing at the sight of Sal.

"She's fuckin' there, Luke." Seth's voice a wet rasp. He's already cracking the passenger-side door, readying to jump out.

Jace is gaping. "Holy shit," he breathes.

That's when Sal glances up. A sob escapes her when she sees the truck. Then she smiles. She surges forward, stumbling slightly, in pain, and still, she moves.

For Luke.

It's the pistol start of his life. He slams on the brakes. He's out of the truck and running. Racing for her.

Sirens fill the air, minutes away. Heartbeats.

Luke's barely aware of his surroundings. Of Seth next to him, in a run, charging toward her.

But then the cabin's front door slams open.

Sal's expression of relief turns to terror.

It's Chris. His leg covered in blood, his face red and twisted, a knife in his hand.

His and Sal's paths converging.

And Luke's far away, still too damn far away.

"Sal!" Luke yells.

She whirls as Chris runs at her. In horror, Luke watches as he angles the knife at Sal's abdomen. Quick, she jumps back, cradling her stomach with her arms. Her ragged cry pierces the air as the blade slices deep into her arm.

Chris tries again. Sal staggers backwards. Tired now, fading, trapped.

A loud bleat of a horn cuts the air.

Chris turns, blinking, surprised by the sound.

A quick glance at each other, then Luke and Seth both split directions. Like when they're on stage, they're in sync, so fucking in sync, so that when Luke grabs up Sal, Seth, using the opportunity created by Jace, explodes past Luke and slams into Chris. He rams them shoulder to shoulder, sending them and the knife sprawling into the dirt and the weeds.

"*Motherfucker,*" Seth snarls, landing a knockout punch to the jaw before Chris can get his bearings.

Sal twists in Luke's arms, craning to see over his shoulder. "Seth…"

"He's okay," Luke says, but concern for his brother has his gaze darting from Sal to Seth, then back to her.

That seems to still Sal, and she goes limp, collapsing to her knees on the ground. Luke goes down with her, immediately pulling her into his arms. She twists into him, burying her face against Luke's chest. Her hands grip the front of his shirt as if hanging on for dear life.

For just a moment, Luke closes his eyes, weak with relief, the feel of Sal finally back in his arms like a goddamn grace.

At the sound of commotion, Luke looks back in time to see Seth and Jace standing over Chris, who's unconscious on the grass. Luke's jaw clenches, murderous rage roiling through him. He aches to go over there and beat the shit out of the guy, but he ain't got it in him. Not when he's got Sal.

Slowly, Luke pulls back, trying to get a good look at her, trying to see what's been done to her. Gently, he palms her shoulders, running his hands over the lump on her temple, the blood streaming down the side of her face. "Sal, let me look at you. Are you hurt?"

"No, no, no, no." The raw words come out like a chant, like a promise she makes to herself. Her eyes are closed, her arms wrapped around herself, her breath a tremor that shakes her tense body.

Seth appears, kneeling beside them, his face pale as he surveys Sal. He swears. "She's bleedin', Luke."

At the sound of Seth's low rumble, Sal's eyes flash open.

"Seth…" Twisting in Luke's arms, she reaches for Seth's

face, blinking like he's a mirage, and his hand trembles, curling around hers to grip it tight.

"I'm okay," he murmurs, placing a palm on the back of her dark head. "Let Luke look at you."

Sal nods. She starts shaking again, shivering like it's winter.

Gently, Luke unfurls her arm. He winces. The cut on her arm's deep. She'll need stitches. And then he remembers what Chris was really aiming for, and he almost can't get air.

"Here," Seth says, shrugging out of his flannel overshirt. He grins, keeping his voice low and soothing. "You keep takin' the shirt off my back, I'm gonna be naked pretty damn soon."

Sal smiles faintly.

Carefully, Luke gathers Sal to him, cradling her in his arms as Seth wraps his shirt around her forearm to stop the bleeding. She flinches and squeezes her eyes shut, the only sound out of her a low moan.

Seth glances sharply at Luke, worry burning bright in his eyes.

It's clear Sal's fading, letting go of whatever strength she was fiercely holding on to, her head sliding to one side as she lies limp and still against Luke's chest. Her eyes stare at the sky, blank, empty. Her face is pale, too pale, her body a vicious tremble.

Luke's chest strains with worry, but he stays calm, keeping Sal in his arms, keeping her still and warm.

A flare of red and blue lights, the bleat of sirens.

"Cops are here," Jace announces, glancing over at the two police cruisers zipping in, followed by an ambulance.

Seth rolls his eyes. "Right in the nick of time."

Luke looks up at his best friend. "Nice job with the airhorn."

Jace grins. "Knew I came along for some reason." He lowers his voice. "I dumped the shotgun down the well. Come back for it later."

Luke nods his silent thanks to Jace. The last thing he needs is to get his dumb ass arrested. Especially now.

Glancing down at Sal, Luke grazes a finger against her cheek. "Darlin', an ambulance is here," he says softly. "We're gonna get you checked out, okay?"

Sal's eyes open. Her breathing hitches, turning ragged. "No."

Jace and Seth exchange uncertain glances.

"Sal, you're hurt. You need—"

"No, Luke, you don't understand." She grips his arm with surprising strength. "There's a dog. In the house. He—he protected me—he could be hurt—"

She breaks into a broken sob. Tears track down her dusty cheeks.

Seth puts a hand out, her sobs tearing at him. "Sal, don't cry. I'll get the dog. Okay?" He stands, and after a final, agonized glance at Sal, he lopes toward the house.

Jace takes off too, striding toward the approaching cops.

"Luke." Sal's soft whisper has him glancing down. Her tears have ebbed, and now her green eyes stare up at him. An unspoken conversation passes between them, a ripple of fierce, unfaltering love. In that instant, he knows what she wants to say, knows that she's afraid to say it.

"I know," he whispers, his voice thick. Hot tears fill his eyes, overwhelmed by how close he's nearly come to losing her. "I know about the baby, Sal."

Her eyes widen. "You do?"

"Seth told me."

"I'm sorry," she says haltingly. She shakes her head, her brow crinkling. "I should have told you. I . . . I . . ." Her emerald-green eyes flutter, losing focus, her head lolling in his arms.

"Shhh," he says, stroking her hair. He can see she's hanging on by the barest thread, fighting to stay awake for him. "It's okay, darlin'. Stay still."

She opens her mouth to say something more, but then the paramedics are there, taking Sal from his arms.

"Be careful with her," Luke demands hoarsely as she's whisked away from him.

He shoves himself up, desperate to get back to her, to fight his way through the crowd. He can see Sal, searching for him as she's eased onto a stretcher, a warm blanket tucked around her.

"Luke . . . where's Luke . . . ?" Her shaky voice carries. Her pale arm reaches for him, only to suddenly fall limply to the side. The effort exhausting, Sal lets out a barely audible sigh and then goes very still on the stretcher, finally giving in to the dark fog of unconsciousness.

Luke closes his eyes.

Let her be okay, he thinks, unable to consider any other alternative. *Let them both be okay.*

THIRTEEN

LUKE'S GOT WEAK KNEES IN THE WAITING ROOM. He's been kept from Sal. They wheeled her in quick and urgent, Luke fighting to stay by her side, but he was ultimately barred from her room. A fact that has him threatening to go flat out insane pretty damn soon.

His eyes jump to the muted television high in the corner of the room. The early morning news ticker screams: *Kidnapping Suspect Apprehended . . . Sal Kincaid Is Safe . . . Brothers Kincaid—Country Superstars or Superheroes? . . . Whirlwind Night of Terror Ends . . .*

A whirlwind night is fucking right.

The cops have long since left. An hour ago, the hospital was crawling with them, lobbing questions at Luke and Seth. But a stern talking-to is all they got from the cops, the Nashville PD apparently deciding making an example of them wasn't the wisest course of action. Now, the cops are gone, and there's a media swarm outside the hospital. Reporters from the *Star* camped out in the parking lot. Chaos incarnate.

Luke hates 'em, but he also owes 'em.

A miracle—it's a miracle he had found her.

His heart leaps at the sound of footsteps coming down the hall. But it's only Seth. Looking about as tired as Luke. His brother's taken over the role of messenger, calling the house, their parents, Lacey, to report back that Sal's been found.

Seth settles beside him. "Anything?"

"Nothin.'" Luke smears a hand down his face. "Christ, I hate waitin.'"

"Yeah, well, while you wait . . ." Seth slaps a vending machine sandwich in his hand.

He glances down. "What do you want me to do with this?"

"Eat somethin.' You're no good to Sal runnin' on fumes."

Numbly, Luke stares at the sandwich. The last thing he feels like doing is eating. He just needs to see Sal.

His chest tightens as fear and panic take up residence. Christ. What if something's wrong? It's been too long. Too damn long without word. Without him right there beside her.

Luke pushes out the words. "I just want them safe."

Seth squeezes his shoulder. He swallows hard. "They will be."

But still, guilt, sorrow claw at him.

"I should've done more," he says. He stares at Sal's hospital room door, the ache in his chest intensifying. It ain't his fault, but hell if it doesn't feel like it. He could've lost her. Again.

Seth gives him a pointed look. One that tells him he'll take him out back and kick his ass if he keeps talking stupid. "Luke, you sounded the alarms before anyone. You knew and you did something. Sal's safe because of you."

"They have to be . . ." Luke lets his words hang unfinished as he runs a trembling hand through his hair. He can't entertain any other options. A life without Sal . . . it won't happen. Not ever again.

Silence falls in the hallway.

A soft click of a lock, the swing of a door. Dr. McKibbon, a familiar face, steps out of Sal's room.

Seth swears, his nerves on edge.

Luke whisks his hands together, his throat knotting. His heartbeat quickens. "What's it gonna be, doc?"

"Everyone's perfect." She smiles. Luke and Seth both let out simultaneous breaths of relief. "No signs of distress in mama or baby."

Seth smirks. "What about the father?"

Luke shoots him a dry look.

Dr. McKibbon opens the door. "Want to come in and see your baby on the big screen?"

For a long second, Luke stands frozen in his boots. As if unable to process the words. Unable to trust the truth. But it's here, in front of him. The fact that they get to do this again. They have another chance.

Beside him, Seth's grinning. He slaps Luke on the back, pushing him forward. "Go, man. Go see your kid."

Luke turns to say thank you, to say that he couldn't do this without him, but his brother's already walking down the hall backwards, his arms outstretched. "Tell Sal I love her. Tell her she owes me. Big-time. Because now I got a goddamn dog to deal with." His laugh lights up the hallway. "I mean it, man, I'm droppin' the damn thing off on your doorstep."

Luke sits beside Sal's bed, her hand clasped in his.

She stares back at him with heavy-lidded but content eyes. Dark hair fanned across her pillow. Bruise on her temple. Her forearm stitched back together and heavily bandaged. She's exhausted, but okay. She's been put through every test under the sun and she came out with a clean bill of health.

Thank Christ.

Luke doesn't know what he did to get so damn lucky, but he's ready to repay whoever, whenever possible.

Dr. McKibbon wheels over the ultrasound machine. "We already ran all the tests to make sure there's no danger to the baby, no premature contractions or abruption, but Sal thought you might want to take a peek for yourself."

His chest constricts. "Yeah, I would."

Dr. McKibbon covers Sal with a sheet and pulls up the hospital gown. There's a squirt of jelly, and then the wand is moving back and forth across Sal's bare stomach.

"Let's see . . . last time we did this, the little one was down here . . ." The wand pauses near Sal's hip bone. McKibbon presses deeper.

Sal smiles.

A low sound like the thunder of a hundred galloping horses fills the room. Luke leans forward in wonder, his throat bobbing. The heartbeat. He hasn't heard it since Henry, but the sound's unmistakable. And so is the image he glimpses on the screen. A head, arms, legs.

A baby. Their baby.

Sal squeezes Luke's hand.

"Goddamn," he says softly. He never thought this would happen again. So many nights of tears and doubt, and now here they are, just like that, their road changed.

"We have a healthy, happy, and probably"—Dr. McKibbon gives Sal a wry glance—"very strong baby."

Sal laughs.

There's a lump in Luke's throat. Hard to talk. Hard to do anything but stare at Sal in awe. He's so damn proud of her. She put herself on the line to help someone else. And she protected herself and their baby to make it back to him. His heart clenches.

She's gonna be the best mother. She's also going to give him a heart attack at the rate she's going.

Sal turns her head, her gaze catching his. Her eyes glitter with unshed tears. Luke brings her hand to his mouth and kisses it.

Dr. McKibbon cleans up Sal and the wand and turns off the machine. She smiles. "I'll give the two of you some privacy." She raises an eyebrow. "I take it you're sleepin' over, Luke."

He grins, his joy so big it could burst. "Wild horses, Doctor."

She chuckles. "I'll send up a cot."

And then they're alone.

"Hi," Sal whispers.

Luke scoots the chair closer, palming her small hand in his. "Hey, yourself, darlin.'"

Without further words, their eyes search each other's. They've barely had time to talk since he got her back, and yet, there's no need for words.

Sal's green eyes, glittering like emeralds, bid him closer.

Letting out a shaky exhale, Luke leans in. His hand slips beneath her dark hair, his lips gently meeting hers. She lets out a little cry but cleaves him closer, her nails digging into his shoulders. She pulls him onto the bed, beside her, and together, they stay like that, tangled in love, in heartbeats. Basking in the wonder of having found each other again, of being together once more.

Finally, Luke breaks the kiss with a tremulous shudder. He touches his forehead to hers. "Christ," he breathes. "I was so damn scared, Sal. So fuckin' afraid."

"I know. I was too." She reaches up to cup his jaw. "You were so brave, Luke. Coming for me like you did."

"I wasn't brave." The words are raw, guttural. "I was weak, Sal. I went weak when I couldn't find you. Thinkin' I could have lost you again . . . it was too damn much, darlin.'"

She shakes her head. "No, you were brave." Her voice is soft with a love, with a strength he's never heard before in his life. "Because I knew. I just knew you'd come for me."

Luke stares down at her, loving her more than he's ever loved her. Her faith, her belief in him, never fails to shake him.

As he gently settles Sal back down in the pillows, her brow crinkles in confusion. "Wait, how *did* you find me?"

"Molly," he says. "She came to the house. Told us where you were."

Sal sighs. "Is she okay?"

His gaze slides to the bandage on her arm. "She's fine, Sal. Thanks to you."

Her throat bobs. "And Chris?"

"Jail," he says with lethal quiet. "For a long goddamn time."

As Luke was climbing into the ambulance beside Sal, he saw Chris being led away in cuffs. It took all Luke had not to leave Sal's side and launch the son of a bitch into the sun.

He reaches out to touch her, taking her hand into his. "I hate that you went through that. After what you've been through . . ."

Her mouth tightens at the thought. Her eyes cloud with emotion as she thinks about it, then she says, "The funny thing is, yes, it was awful and terrifying, but if anyone could handle it, I could." Her eyes grow contemplative. "I'm not glad it happened, but I think I went through the dark the first time so I could survive the second."

His stomach dips at the thought. Imagining Sal taking on that terror again, reliving her monstrous experience with Roy, is enough to get Luke on his knees and keep him there.

Still, she's right. She is.

She's endured the worst of so many things and survived. The thought doesn't reassure him. It doesn't make him want to protect her any less, and he'll never stop, but neither will she. She's a force, his wife, and whoever fucks with her fucks with him.

He brings her hand to his mouth, pressing a kiss to her palm, her tattoo.

Sal inhales a breath, tilting her dark head. "Are you happy, Luke?" Her face is hesitant, hopeful. "About the baby?"

"Am I—" Luke breaks off, his eyes wide. He straightens, trying to find the words for what this means to him. What they mean to him. "Sal, I'm over the goddamn moon." He cups her face and she leans into his palm, her cheek as soft as a petal. "It was a surprise, that's for sure. But a goddamn great one. I just—why didn't you tell me?"

"I didn't want you to be disappointed again." She swallows and meets his gaze. "I overheard you and Seth talking on the porch about how hard it's been for you. I didn't know how much you were hurting. When I found out about the baby, I wanted to protect you like you've protected me." Her eyes fall to her stomach. "I was planning to tell you last night." She purses her lips, lets out a wry laugh. "Although, this wasn't exactly how I wanted you to find out."

He nods slowly as her words sink in, understanding rippling through him at how she put him first. Goddamn, how he loves her.

Sal's eyes, heavy with sleep, stare into his, all kinds of solemn. "I love you, Luke."

In response, Luke rests a hand over her stomach.

The only sound is the faint beeping of the heart monitors. The baby's and Sal's.

All he needs.

The most perfect harmony he's ever heard.

Sal smiles at the late-afternoon sunlight coming in the window. Somehow, mysteriously, magically, flowers have appeared while she was sleeping. Big, gorgeous bouquets that feel as sunny as she does. Her room is bustling with people, which has her husband's handsome face pulled into a dark scowl.

Luke, his arms crossed, keeps a tall and protective watch over her bed while she speaks to the cops, answering their cut-and-dried questions. They've been here for nearly an hour and she knows it's only a matter of time before they get booted.

While the cops finish up, nurses check her pulse and blood pressure. They want to monitor her and the baby for another few hours before she's discharged. Though the swelling on her temple has gone down, her arm's on fire thanks to painkillers being off-limits.

She'll take it, though.

She'll take every shitty and great and wondrous thing this pregnancy will bring.

The detective, a calm man with muttonchops, stares down at her as he stands. "If you think of anything else, you call us."

She nods, her hands keeping a protective clasp around her belly. "I will."

The door cracks. Seth slides into the room, a bag of coffee in his hands, a steady stream of cacophony following him in. He gives Luke a look as he shuts the door. "*Star*'s camped out at the exit. Fuckers. We toss 'em one damn bone and they ain't lettin' go."

Luke turns to peer out the window, his brow furrowed.

Seth goes to Sal, perching on the edge of her bed. His eyes take her in, the bruise on her cheek, the bandage on her arm, the heart monitors keeping watch on her and the baby.

He leans down to kiss her. "You look awful."

She laughs. "Thanks a lot."

"I brought you coffee." He grins. "Figured you had enough flowers."

Sal eyes the bag of dark roast and smiles. "Figured right."

The detective pauses at the door and clears his throat. "Oh, and one more thing, Mr. Kincaid. We heard somethin' about a shotgun on the scene."

The news is new to her, causing Sal's breath to hitch, her body to go taut. Worry stokes in her at the stern look the cop's giving Luke.

"Your shotgun," the cop goes on, eyeing Luke closely.

Thinking on it, Luke gives a swift shake of his head. Keeping an easy tone, fingers hooked around his belt buckle, he looks to his brother. "Can't say I recall. Seth?"

Seth shrugs. "Nothin' rings a bell."

Whether the cop doesn't care or doesn't believe him, Sal can't tell. All he does is give a curt nod and then exits without a backwards glance.

Sal's lungs expand and she can breathe again.

There's a loud exhale from Seth. He locks eyes with his brother and then laughs. "Hell, I'm callin' Jace," he says, standing. "Just in case. Trust that guy to be the one to get our asses arrested. He's got a damn conscience."

Before he can leave, Sal grabs Seth's hand and pulls him down. "Thank you."

It's all she can say. Gratitude pumps through her veins. So much appreciation, so much gratefulness he had Luke's back, that he kept her secret the best he could, that he came for her.

"You get better, you hear?" He sweeps a lock of hair out of her eyes, his voice a soft rumble of a drawl. "You're kinda my favorite person, so you gotta stick around. But don't tell Luke. It'll break his heart."

A scoff from Luke.

Sal smiles. "Feeling's mutual."

Seth looks at Luke. "I'll see you later."

Luke nods.

When Seth's gone, Luke sits in a chair beside her bed, his long fingers curling around hers as he scoops up her hand.

Sal's eyes narrow. "What were you gonna do with that shotgun, Luke?"

He meets her gaze, nothing but granite-tough strength in his words. "Whatever I had to do."

A ripple of worry. "What if the cops—"

"No one's gettin' arrested, darlin'," Luke reassures, scanning her face. "I did what I had to do to bring you home. Ain't nothin' to worry about, so don't."

A spark of love hits her hard, Sal marveling at just what lengths he'd go to for her.

Lifting her hand, she cups his strong jaw. "Country boy, you trying to play bodyguard?"

His eyes flash. "For you, you're goddamn right."

She stares at him, undone. By their love. By their baby. By Luke's lean hand, his tan fingers fanned out protectively over her stomach.

The door cracks.

Luke glances over, his expression irritated. But the tightness in his face eases at the flash of red hair. "Hi," Alabama says, stepping inside with Griff. "We just wanted to peek in on y'all. Seth said it'd be okay."

"Of course," Sal says softly.

Alabama hurries over, trading places with Luke, who goes to Griff.

"Good Lord, Sal," Alabama drawls, giving her a light hug. "You sure gave us a scare."

"How are you doin', sweetheart?" Griff asks, peering close at Sal as he shakes hands with Luke.

"Tired, sore." She laughs a little. "I should be out of here later today," Sal says, casting a sideways glance at her husband. "Although if Luke had his way, I'd probably be here for the next week."

"Try the next month," he volleys.

Sal rolls her eyes.

Alabama stares at Sal, a bright beam of a smile curving her lips. "I hear congratulations are in order."

Sal ducks her head and laughs. "Yeah. Yeah, they are."

"'Bout time this day finally ended in some damn good news." Griff slaps Luke hard on the back and lets out a wild hoot. "We gotta celebrate, Kincaid."

"We damn sure will." Luke grins, his entire face a light of joy. "When we get home."

As his warm, dark eyes land on Sal, she shivers.

Home.

She places a palm on her stomach.

They're all going home.

chapter
FOURTEEN

LUKE FLICKS ON THE BEDSIDE LIGHT, LETTING IT burn as he helps Sal crawl into their plush bed. She collapses into the pillow, snuggling deep and letting out a content sigh. Before Luke can turn away to draw the blinds, she catches his arm. "Stay," she says, her eyes already closed.

He smiles. "Sleep, Sal." He kisses her cheek, wincing as he thumbs a finger across her bruised brow. "I want you restin.'"

"Stay," she whispers, her husky voice breathy and light. But within seconds, she's asleep, her dark hair haloed around her head.

Gently, he tucks the sheet around her slender frame, around the soft cotton T-shirt and jersey sleep shorts. When he's satisfied she's comfortable, Luke sits on the end of the bed, taking in the light rise and fall of Sal's chest. The very sight of her finally sleeping easy a comfort.

He sighs, smearing his face in his hands. Sleep—it's what he should be doing. Because it's been a goddamn day. Between getting Sal out of the hospital and fighting the paparazzi vying for her photo and issuing a press statement thanking the *Nashville Star* for their help, he's never been more exhausted.

Never been happier.

His wife is back at home. Safe.

Luke bristles at the sound of the front door opening and closing, then frowns. He listens. Hard boot steps in sync with the frantic skitter of claws.

He fights a laugh as Seth appears in the upstairs hallway. He groans and leans forward, resting elbows on the knees of his jeans. "You didn't."

Seth leans in the doorway, arms crossed. "Oh, I did."

Luke's eyes drift to the mangy dog standing beside Seth. With a groan, he pushes up. He gives Sal a last look and then exits the bedroom to join Seth in the hallway. He kneels, evaluating the dog and its tags. Luke arcs a brow. "Winston, huh?" He gives the mangy mutt a head scratch. "You ain't no hound dog, but Sal seems to like you, so . . ."

With that, as if he's satisfied with Luke's stamp of approval, the dog wanders into the bedroom and hops onto the bed. He goes to Sal, curling up against her, resting his chin on her thigh. His dark eyes are alert and watchful.

Seth grins. "Looks like you got a dog now."

"Looks like it." Luke crosses his arms, surveys the mutt keeping watch at the end of Sal's bed.

"He ain't so bad," Seth says, clear affection in his voice. "I got him cleaned up for Sal. His bowl and all his other shit is downstairs." His eyes flick to Luke. "Y'all make it out of the hospital okay?"

Luke turns, resting a hip against the banister to look at his brother. He gives a shallow nod, then says, "We're gonna keep the baby quiet as long as we can. They're gonna want photos. I ain't exposin' Sal to that. Not right now."

Seth nods in agreement. His eyes move from Luke to Sal. "I called Lacey. Let her know what's goin' on."

Luke groans, yanking a hand through his hair. "Fuck." In the midst of all the chaos, he had been so focused on Sal, he had forgotten to call Lacey and give her an update on Sal and the baby. "I damn forgot. Thanks. She okay?"

Though he and Lacey have had their issues in the past, they're back to where they used to be. He feels like an ass-hole for inadvertently shutting her out.

Seth shrugs. "Hissed at me a lot. Massive pain in the ass. Said she'll call Sal tomorrow. But yeah, she's okay. "

Frowning, Luke cuts a brief glance to Seth. His broth-er's voice is tight, constricted by an odd tenderness he can't quite place. But before he can say anything, Seth claps him on the shoulder.

"You're gonna be a dad, man." He stares at Luke, his ex-pression mischievous and wondering. "How do you feel?"

A slow smile spreads across Luke's face. "Man . . . I . . . damn." His throat bobs, the gamut of emotions damn near felling him. "I'm lucky."

Seth chuckles. "You're gonna be busy for a while. Got a dog. A baby. The gig next month. The album." He turns toward his brother, grinning. "Shit, Luke. Life's good."

Luke grins back at him. "Life's great."

"Hell, I'm gonna get." Seth floats a last look to Sal, then Luke. "Anything y'all need, whiskey, bourbon, a babysitter, a new shotgun, call."

Luke laughs. "Get outta here." He gives his brother a

look of thanks. "You've done enough." He cocks a brow. "Unless . . ."

Seth barks a laugh and makes for the stairs. "I love ya, man, but I ain't takin' that damn dog back."

Sal finds Luke in the living room, a glass of whiskey in his hand. She smiles, watching unseen from the doorway as he puts on his favorite old-school country record. Hank Williams's mournful warble rings out, filling the living room.

As if sensing her eyes on him, he straightens up. Turns. Sighs. "You're supposed to be sleepin.'"

She crosses her arms, her eyes narrowing. Exhaustion lines his handsome face. "What about you?"

"Oh, I'm runnin' on whiskey." He laughs, holds up his glass. "Then I'm gonna sleep for days."

"Days on days on days," Sal agrees. She's never been so exhausted, but she woke with the space beside her cold, unable to bear it, needing Luke beside her. His warmth, his strength. Her husband.

There's a low woof beside her and Sal kneels, running her fingers through Winston's now-shiny fur. She looks up at Luke. "He's ours?"

He nods, the ice in his whiskey glass clinking. "If you want him."

"I do." She gives Winston a last ruffle of his fur, loving this pup that saved her so fiercely, and then stands.

But Luke's already on his way toward her.

He takes a few long-legged strides across the living

room and she meets him in the middle. He dips to kiss her. Whiskey on his lips, love in his eyes. The kiss is as sweet as a mountain stream and Sal drinks him in.

She pulls away, but Luke keeps her close, cleaved in his warm arms. When he offers her a sip of whiskey, she shakes her head, smiling mischievously up at him. "Don't think we want the baby to get started this early."

"Jesus," he says, his mouth falling open. Adorably earnest. "I damn forgot."

And then Luke laughs and laughs and her heart dances. That laugh. Damn how she loves it. Like firecrackers lighting up the dark. Shaking the old farmhouse awake, sparking every bit of her like a flame.

Loves him, she thinks, her eyes falling appreciatively on his tall, taut form. Luke looks hot as hell even in his disheveled, exhausted state. Tall, tan, lean. Blue jeans and his black T-shirt—there's nothing better for Sal than that.

Swigging down the finger of whiskey, Luke dips to set the glass on the coffee table. But he doesn't let her loose for long, pulling her once again into his arms. His lean, muscular hands bracket her waist, holding her tightly against him.

She buries her head against his chest. "I keep forgetting too." Her mouth curves. "We're gonna be parents."

Luke's arm tightens around her.

Looking up at him, Sal stands on tiptoes, her hands palming his chest. She needs him to hear this, but she also needs to say it aloud. Like a new promise. A different kind of vow for this new place in their life.

"I want you to hear something, Luke."

He nods down at her, his handsome face soft and listening.

"I know we don't know how it will all turn out. I know we'll never have peace of mind, we'll always worry about the baby, about something, but I want us to try, Luke." She takes a breath, hot tears filling her eyes. "Whatever happens, I want us to walk our road without trouble, together. Live every damn second we're alive. Tours. The bus. Our friends and family. I can't remember Henry, but this baby . . . you, our life, it's enough. It's all I need."

Tears shine in Luke's eyes. "God, I love you," he chokes out, cupping her face with trembling hands. "I'm gonna love that baby too, darlin'. With everything I got."

Sal's heart clenches. "I know you will," she whispers. "I love you, Luke. And I love our road."

His throat bobs, his thumb a tender whisk across her cheekbone.

Somewhere in the house, Winston barks.

Sal laughs. "He's checking us out."

Luke chuckles. "He pees in our room, he's sleepin' in the barn."

"He needs love. He's a good dog." Sal moves closer, moves her bare thigh between Luke's legs. Lean legs she knows Luke loves. Legs he can't say no to. "I need love too."

Luke groans, palms her shoulders. "You need rest, Sal." But his dark eyes flash, male lust warring with concern.

"Let's rest together."

His lips quirk. "Darlin', you're merciless."

"How do you think I got so far in life?" She nips his earlobe. "How do you think I got so far with you?"

"That uniform always was your secret weapon."

She bites her lip, her body thrumming. "Kiss me, country boy."

His hands slide up her shoulders to cup her face. Their eyes lock, so much love there, and then he crushes his lips to hers, burning, lit, a fuse and Sal's ready. Ready to chase away the last twenty-four hours without Luke.

Sal curls her fingers in his hair, hard, wrenching, her body aching, arching into him. She moans, pressing her breasts against his chest.

He breaks away with a gasp. "Sal." Her name is guttural, a runaway breath, an on-his-knees plea.

She walks Luke backwards to the couch. When he hits the cushion, he sits, pulling her between his thighs. He grins up at her, then glances down. Almost hesitantly, his long fingers palm her abdomen, and then his face softens and he presses a fervent kiss to her stomach, gripping her hard around the waist.

Love kindles Sal's stomach. She threads her fingers through his dark hair and then yelps in delight as he pulls her into a straddling position on his lap.

She reaches out and cups his chiseled jaw. "I love you, Luke Kincaid."

"You, always," he says, low and raw. And then he takes her slender frame in his strong arms and kisses her. Kisses her like she's his very heartbeat. Kisses her like the world is ending.

No, never. Not for them.

Their road burns bright before her, and Sal melts into Luke.

His kiss has roots, lifelong, flowing through Sal to the warm home of her heart.

There are no more words for this, for them.

She's survived. Luke's survived. Together, they've

conquered their demons and found their way back to each other again and again and again.

And soon . . .

As Luke sweeps his lips across hers, a shiver of anticipation runs down Sal's spine.

Soon, they'll tell their friends and family about the baby. But for now, she and Luke get this moment.

This new forever road for the two of them to walk together.

chapter
ONE

THROW IT AWAY. *JUST FLUSH IT DOWN THE FUCKIN'* *drain, man.*

The voice inside Seth Kincaid's head is insistent, damn near on a tear. But he doesn't listen. He can't. Instead, he sits on his couch staring at the baggie of white powder, his vision blurry from alcohol, from tears, wondering if he's got anything left to live for anymore. Wondering if everyone back at the hospital hates his sorry, pathetic ass.

Because he sure as hell does.

Because if anything happens to his brother, he'll never forgive himself.

"Fuck," Seth says, shoving at the coffee table. He falls back against the couch and rips a hand through his hair. Contemplates a dangerous habit he hasn't touched in over ten years. Snorting down a reckless line of white powder, searching for that slow sink into numb oblivion.

That's all he wants to do. Forget.

Last night.

The image of Jace and Griff practically carrying a grief-stricken Sal to Luke's hospital room.

Seth leans forward. He wants to make a mistake. Make the awful feeling in his heart go away.

The baggie's heavy in his hand. A distraction, a death wish, he doesn't know. But he could find out. He wants to find out. Wants to go back to ten years ago, make his OD permanent, make his dumbass-self null and void.

He squeezes his eyes shut.

Luke.

His brother's the glue that holds their family together. The backbone of the band. How can they live without Luke? It should have been him. Not Luke. Never.

A pounding on the door has him opening his eyes. "Go away," Seth shouts, waving his arm in what he thinks is the direction of the sound.

But the knocking's insistent, grating.

Gritting his teeth, he shoves off the couch, wading through his drunken haze, stumbling for the door. When he gets there, he braces a hand on the doorframe. Briefly, he watches the room spin. Then he squares his shoulders and yanks open the door.

The blast of icy air hits him hard, and he isn't talking about the chilly September night.

Lacey Sutton stands there, arms crossed, a scowl on her pretty face. Her blonde hair falls around her shoulders like corn silk.

"Go away," he repeats, though he doesn't know if she heard him the first time.

She lifts her chin, haughty. Not bothering with a hello, she says, "You left the hospital, Seth. You left Sal. And. . ." She sniffs the air, levels him with a decisive eye. Her nostrils flare. "You're drunk."

He damn sure is drunk. Earlier tonight, he fled the hospital for the nearest bar. He couldn't handle the conversation or the scene. Everyone sitting on hard plastic chairs, waiting for Luke to wake up, wondering, worrying about a brain bleed. Sal, holding hands with Jace, never looking at Seth, and it was killing him, not knowing if she blamed him.

When he returned, five strong drinks in, Lacey was there. He doesn't remember how he got back to the hospital. He could barely walk a straight line, let alone piece together what the doctors were saying about Luke's potential head injury. Finally, it was Griff, damn Griff Greyson who had taken him aside. "Go home, Seth, you're scarin' Sal," Griff commanded. But what Seth saw in his eyes wasn't the irritation they usually had for each other.

It was pity.

Seth moves to shut the door on Lacey, but she shoves a long, trim leg into the opening.

"Goddamnit," he swears, stopping the door in time from crushing her limb. "You ain't comin' in, Lacey."

"I am and I will."

With that, she elbows her way inside.

Seth watches blearily as she blows in like a hurricane, ready to thrash everything in her path, including him.

He groans, smearing a hand down his face. The click-clack of her high heels are like miniature drills on his brainstem, but instead of leaving like he expects her too, she slams the door and locks it.

Seth hasn't seen Lacey in months. And now she's in Nashville, having flown a red-eye to be with her sister, Sal, during the torturous wait for Luke to wake up. She had arrived tonight and apparently followed him back to his apartment.

Lacey's accusing eyes land on him. "You should be at the hospital. You should be there with Sal, not here ready to sleep off a bender. Luke needs you, Seth."

He flinches. "I ain't in the mood, Lacey."

Lacey props her hands on her tapered waist. She knows where his mind has gone and it's nowhere good. "You know it's not your fault, right?"

"Did Sal say that?" he asks bitterly. "Or hell, maybe Jace asked you to come by, smack some sense into me."

She sighs. Her mouth turned down into an unhappy scowl. "*I* know what happened and *I'm* the one saying it's not your fault."

But it is his fault.

He nearly got his brother killed. Him and his big fat fucking mouth.

It's been years since Seth started a fight, let alone lost his temper at a gig. But two nights ago, down on Broadway, he did.

Seth braces himself against the memory, but he's helpless to stop it. It's a freight train approaching, and he's right in the goddamn way.

The Brothers Kincaid, plus Sal, were in the bar, grabbing a drink before their show. A couple of rednecks in a corner booth were talking shit about their band, about Sal. Luke wouldn't start a fight, especially with Sal there, but Seth didn't have the same high standards as his brother. He's a nice guy, but you fuck with his family and all bets are off.

So, he shot his mouth off about something he can't even remember now. When the fight threatened to get physical, Luke stepped in, trying to diffuse the situation, trying to talk everyone down. Arms up, hands out, he had said to the redneck, "Hey, man, we don't want any trouble. Let's just call it and go our separate ways."

They all agreed. But when Luke turned to walk away, the redneck cracked him across the back of the head with a beer bottle.

His brother stood stunned, then he fell.

And Sal —

Sal screamed, her voice shredding on Luke's name, some awful, unearthly sound, as she collapsed to her knees. Her hands hovered around Luke's head. The blood on her hands as bright as a spotlight.

All Seth could do was stare at his brother's lifeless body lying in a pool of blood.

Then he snapped.

Fists flying, he was on the redneck so fast he could have killed him. He nearly did. "Motherfucker, you are a dead man," he hissed before Jace dragged him off the guy.

From there, it was a blur. The ambulance, the hospital, the *Nashville Star*, the police and their questions, everyone gathering, coming for Luke.

If Seth would've listened to Luke and walked away, then his brother wouldn't be in a hospital bed right now, hurt, unconscious, god knows what else.

His fault. All his goddamned fault.

"Seth?"

Lacey's soft voice floats over him, pulling him from his memories.

Seth blinks, his mind foggy. When he looks up, all he

sees is the light of the moon shining through the window and her thin silhouette.

He turns away from her, not wanting her to witness him at his lowest. "You gotta go, princess. Go on, get outta here."

She doesn't budge. Any other person he'd kick their ass out, but he knows he doesn't move Lacey.

He trudges to the couch and sits down. Time to make his mind a big, blank slate.

Lacey opens her mouth to yell at him, but the snappish retort drops from her lips. Her green eyes light on the coffee table, the bag of powder.

Slowly, she crosses the room and lowers herself beside him on the couch.

"Oh my god, Seth. Where'd you get this?" Her face horrified, Lacey reaches over him, so close he can smell her lavender and sea salt scent. A scent that shouldn't be so familiar, shouldn't smell so damn good, but does. When she snags the bag from the coffee table, his stomach twists. The sight of her holding something so dangerous has him trembling.

He grabs her hand. "Don't."

She stares at him.

Instead of extricating her fingers, she twines them with his, the baggie caught between their palms like a kind of temporary jail. Her hands are warm, her touch like a torch.

"You can't." Her whisper cuts the silence between them.

He swallows. "I have to."

"No, Seth. You don't."

He squeezes his eyes shut, hot tears burning his lids. His throat bobs. "I need you."

Those three simple words have her face softening.

"I know," she says.

And then her hand, delicate, graceful, removes itself from his. The bag disappears, where he doesn't know, and then Lacey's cupping his scruffy cheek. Her face so damn beautiful, so kind, it has him choking up. "I'm here, Seth. Okay?"

It breaks him. Her words, her offer, like some heaven-sent angel.

"Oh god," Seth cries out, pressing a hand to his eyes. Every emotion spilling over inside of him. Guilt, love, pain. His greatest fear. Something happening to Luke. His best friend. His bandmate. His brother. His *fucking* brother.

"If Luke ain't okay—"

"He is, he will be," Lacey soothes. She holds Seth close, sweeping tears from his face.

Seth sobs.

Sal and Luke had been through so much. Luke had just learned that he was going to be a father. Without Luke, without him singing beside Seth on that stage, it's all hollow. His life means nothing.

Lacey lowers herself to her knees beside him. Seth wraps his arms around her waist. He grips her tight and buries his head against her stomach. "It's my fault. It's all my fault."

Shushing him, she leans down. She kisses the back of his head softly, her palm making smooth, healing caresses over his spine.

He raises his face.

Caught by an impulse, that same impulse that keeps getting him in trouble, he kisses her. His lips meet hers for the first time in months, soft and sweet, damn near desperate. He clutches her to him. Better than any drug.

His escape, his release, his goddamn savior.

When he goes to stop himself, to end their kiss, to pull his hand from her blonde hair, it's too late. He can't. He never could.

But then Lacey pulls away with a small gasp, leaving the chalk outline of her kiss on his lips. Her slender hands cradle his face. Her breath a pulse against his. "We can't," she whispers. "Not like this."

Even as he shakes his head in protest, he knows she's right. Blearily, he wonders when it changed, when they've gone from a sometimes-fling to this. When they keep saying *not-anymore*, only *not-anymore* keeps turning into *I-need-you-now*.

"I'm sorry," he mumbles.

She presses her cheek against his. "Don't be."

With a quick sweep of her hand, she palms the drug, a drug he never should have touched, and then the girl he never should have kissed is standing, swishing down the hall, delicate footsteps, a flourish of silk, the flush of a toilet, and then Lacey's back, returning to him, no drug in sight, a glass of water in her hands.

Once again, she sits beside him.

In that moment, Seth's hit with a hot rush of shame at the thought of what he's done.

Ten years ago, he promised Luke he'd never touch the stuff again, and what did he do? He broke that promise to both him and Sal. He failed the people he loves most in this world.

"Fuck," he moans, burying his face in his hands. "You can't tell, Luke. You can't ever tell him."

"I won't." Lacey's eyes blaze with fire. With protection. "He'll never know, Seth."

He nods, dumbly, alcohol clouding his vision, his thoughts. He smears a hand across his face, needing to pull himself together, but he can't think. Exhaustion has him.

Lacey takes his shoulder, gripping hard with her manicured nails, and pulls him against her. The two of them lay back on the couch, Lacey's arms wrapped tight around him.

"You'll be okay," she says, her voice as fierce as Seth's ever heard. "I won't let you be anything else. Do you hear me?"

"I don't care about me," he chokes out. "Tell me he'll be okay."

"I care about you." Lacey kisses his brow. "And he'll be okay."

"Tell me until I believe, Lace."

"Luke will be okay. He will be okay."

She repeats it, like a vow, over and over again until her soft voice lulls Seth.

He closes his eyes at the feel of her thin fingers sweeping through his hair. He wants to tell her thank you, tell her he couldn't make it through tonight without her, but he's asleep before he finds the words to tell her what she means to him.

Coming July 2022

books by

AVA HUNTER

The Nashville Star Series
Sing You Home
Find You Again
Love You Always
Need You Now
Bring You Back

acknowledgments

Thank you for reading *Love You Always*! Special thanks to Eliza Dee for the edits and Sarah Hansen for the gorgeous cover. My beta readers—Christina and Tammie—thank you. Thank you to all the readers and bloggers and bookstagrammers who read and spread the word about my books. And last but not least, thank you to my friends and family for putting up with my writerly angst. You know you love it. And I love you.

Ava Hunter is a strong believer in black coffee, red wine, and the there's-only-one-bed trope. She writes contemporary romance with healthy amounts of angst, where the damsels are never quite damsels, but the men they love (good, bad and rugged) are always there for them. Her first series, *Nashville Star*, centers on sexy country singers and their honky-tonk drama-filled lives. When Ava isn't parked in front of the computer writing, she is mom-ing, reading, traveling, drinking wine, baking and watching good TV. She writes from her home in Arizona, where she lives with her husband, daughter, and a very chonky cat.